It
Takes
You
Over

©2012 by Nick Healy
First Edition
Library of Congress Control Number: 2011942067
ISBN: 978-0-89823-263-9
eISBN: 978-0-89823-279-0
Many Voices Project #125

Cover design by Kayla Reinholz
Interior design by Daniel A. Shudlick

The publication of *It Takes You Over* is made possible by the generous support of the McKnight Foundation and other contributors to New Rivers Press.

For academic permission or copyright clearance please contact Frederick T. Courtright at 570-839-7477 or permdude@eclipse.net.

New Rivers Press is a nonprofit literary press associated with Minnesota State University Moorhead.

Alan Davis, Co-Director and Senior Editor
Suzzanne Kelley, Co-Director and Managing Editor
Wayne Gudmundson, Consultant
Allen Sheets, Art Director
Thom Tammaro, Poetry Editor
Kevin Carollo, MVP Poetry Coordinator

Publishing Interns:
David DeFusco, Andreana Gustafson, Katelin Hansen, Noah M. Kleckner, Daniel A. Shudlick, Sarah Z. Sleeper, Alicia Strnad

It Takes You Over Book Team:
Emily Enger, Jamee Larson, Justin Montgomery

New Rivers Press
c/o MSUM
1104 7th Avenue South
Moorhead, MN 56563
www.newriverspress.com

It Takes You Over

Over

Stories by Nick Healy

For
H.E.H.

Contents

1	Joyless Men
19	Ashes and Spit
37	The Baroness
67	Close Relations
89	The Deep Route
107	And Other Delights
123	Not Funny
145	Lives of Great Northerners
165	Squirt
175	Uncle Ed's Packard

Acknowledgments
Author Biography

Joyless Men

The telephone woke me just after midnight. I figured the call could only be one of two things—bad news or a wrong number—and wanted to ignore it. But I rolled across the side of the bed once occupied by my wife and plucked the receiver from the nightstand, where she used to keep a pile of books about how to better enjoy life. I cleared my throat and said hello.

"Forgive me for calling, Carl." The voice on the other end came through slowly and quietly. "This is Peter Johnson."

"Pete?"

"Johnson," he said, "Mary's husband."

"Pete, I know who you are." The Johnsons had been our neighbors for almost twenty years, and they'd lived on Simpson Street for ten years before we came along. Everyone on the block knew them by name and by sight—the fat lady and the stick man—and knew that Mary had gone off to a nursing home last year.

"Fine," he said. "I could use your help about now."

"I'm half asleep, Pete. It's the middle of the night. What's the trouble?"

It was true that neither Pete nor Mary had ever been anything but kind to me, my wife Nan, and our two girls. They were good neighbors. They kept a spare key for us, picked up our papers when we'd gone up north, and reminded us to get our leaves out to the curb a day before the city crew was scheduled to come and take them away.

It was also true that I had said cruel things about Pete and his wife, that I had looked at them through our windows and uttered whatever coarse jokes came to mind. When Mary took their gray terrier Linus for a walk, I compared the leash to a tether on the great Hindenburg, destined to explode before stunned onlookers. I suggested Pete and Linus were on borrowed time, that eventually Mary would get hungry enough to eat them, too. And I took to calling Pete's wife Maryland, the woman whose ass was large enough to merit statehood.

Our girls, always immobile in front of the television in our living room, didn't often laugh at my gags, but they latched onto the nickname. Everyone in our house—even my wife, who accused me of being crude and unkind—used it in our private conversations. The girls spread it to other neighborhood kids, and I assume those kids brought it home to their parents. My wife worried that Pete or Mary would find out. She tried to get us all to stop saying it, but the day they took Pete's wife away, Nan called me at the office and said, "Maryland had a stroke. It took four paramedics to carry her out of the house."

I pulled a pair of blue jeans and a heavy sweater over my flannel pajamas. In the foyer, I zipped my parka snug to my chin, picked up my keys, and hurried outside. I'd promised Pete I could get to the city lockup in fifteen minutes, no more than twenty.

Snow, packed hard on the front walk, groaned and cracked beneath the rubber soles of my boots. Each step produced a clean and loud sound like the snapping of a thick twig, which echoed down the block and bounced off the dark houses.

I worried that the racket of my minivan—the roar from its rusted muffler and the whine of its cold belts—might wake the neighbors, and some of my wife's cronies might peek out to see me driving off and then whisper to her about my strange comings and goings in the middle of the night, hound-dogging around town with God only knows who.

The streets were empty in our neighborhood and mostly the same when I crossed into St. Paul, cut through Como Park, and headed downtown. This sort of cold kept people, including the riffraff, off the streets. I figured that had made Pete an easy mark for the cops, who were probably bored half stiff even in the middle of Frogtown, long the part of the city where people went looking for unlawful thrills. That was where Pete had gotten into his trouble. On the phone he hadn't been forthcoming with the details. He said only that the police had stopped him with some "young lady" in his car.

Once the van warmed up, I didn't mind being out. The world looks different when the temperature drops so far below zero. Everything takes on a crispness and tidiness. Salt and slush harden into a dry white film on the asphalt. The glow of each streetlight forms a distinct umbrella. The trails of smoke from chimneys and tailpipes swirl in tight curls and then disappear. To be out in that weather—when all other creatures had hidden themselves away—made me feel bold and strong, even though I rode inside the warm shell of a rumbling machine.

I tried to imagine Pete searching for a Frogtown pro—that's what most lonely guys went down there for—but it didn't add up. I envisioned him rolling down his window to talk to the girl and a rush of cold air swooshing in, stirring his nerves and causing him to fumble with words. The Pete I knew wouldn't have had the first idea what to say, how to go about it.

Lots of people have secret lives, little parts of themselves they keep hidden away, but Pete wasn't the sort of guy to be cruising Frogtown. I knew that in the way I knew he loved Maryland, that he had never once been embarrassed by her. I knew because of all those years I had watched them together, noticed the way he looked at her, and heard how he spoke to her. Pete was good even in his secret places.

When she left a week before Halloween, Nan said she and the girls were going to stay with her mother and that she didn't know when they would be back. When I asked why, she droned a list of the ways I had let her down and made her feel unloved.

"You have become a joyless man, Carl." The girls were waiting in Nan's car when she said this. "Don't you want to change that? Don't you want something better? For yourself, I mean? Or for all of us?"

"We've been together for twenty years," I said. "We had six months of infatuation, but since then, we've been pretty much the same as we are now. That's how couples are. That's how marriage is."

"That's a marriage, huh? You tell me you've been bored for nineteen and a half years, and you expect this to make me feel better?" Nan had her hair in a ponytail like she'd worn all the time back in college, but it was darker now and streaked with gray. "What do you know about marriage?"

We stood in the foyer and stared at each other. Nan had her hand on the doorknob. I thought about reaching out and taking her arm—gently, in a way that would only say that I didn't want her to go. But all I could see in her face and her tired shoulders was the wear of the years, and I couldn't think of a good reason for her to stay.

"I only know what our marriage has taught me," I said. "I thought you knew the same. I thought we were on the same page."

Nan's top lip curled and shivered, and she spoke in bursts. "You know shit. You know shit about marriage. You know shit about me."

She cranked the knob, jerked open the door, and backed over the threshold.

"The same page? That's great, Carl." Her hip held open the storm door. Nan leaned back inside and spoke softly again. "I was never on that page."

The streets of downtown St. Paul always went quiet after business hours, and they were especially so after midnight. The cold and emptiness made the place look unreal—like a painted backdrop at the old Palace Theater, where the marquee was dark when I drove past. The Christmas lights that city workers strung along the boulevards each year had been shut off, too, and no cars were parked outside the jailhouse.

I left my van running and hurried across the sidewalk. A bank sign said the temperature had sunk down near twenty below. The air tightened the skin on my face, hardened the short curls of my beard, dried my sinuses, and jolted my lungs with an energy that felt almost like youth. I slowed near the doorway to look at the stout old towers in that corner of the city. Everything looked clean and sturdy—beautiful, I thought. Still, I couldn't wait to get inside.

The lobby of the jail was dim and cramped, not at all like I had expected, and it reeked of microwave popcorn. A young cop—a woman—sat alone behind a counter. No one else was around. The officer's name badge said "Vang." She held up one finger, smiled with tight lips, chewed a few times, and swallowed.

"Sir," she said. "You can't leave your van running out there."

I glanced back at the doorway, wondering how the hell she'd know that, and gave her a curious look. She tapped her finger on top of the closed-circuit monitor on her desk.

"I'll only be a minute," I said. "I've come for Peter Johnson, my neighbor. How do I get him sprung from this place?"

"You can't leave an unattended vehicle on the street with the motor running."

Officer Vang was a pretty and tiny thing with smooth skin on her cheeks and eyes of the darkest brown. They were knowing eyes for someone so young. She couldn't have been older than twenty-three or twenty-four.

"Oh, it'll be okay," I said. "What sort of a nut would try to steal a vehicle from outside the jail?"

"The kind who'd rather nab a nice warm piece of junk than spend the night freezing to death outside." She smiled again, wider this time, and I could see a small flake of popcorn hull wedged in her lower teeth.

"Look," I said. "Pete—my neighbor—has had a rough night already, and he's an older guy. It would be nice for him to get into a warm car, don't you think? Maybe you'd keep lookout for me?"

She rolled her eyes, pressed a button on her desk, and nodded toward the door over her shoulder. I walked to the door and thanked her before I headed into the back.

"I take no responsibility for that van," Officer Vang said.

It was true there was a good reason for Nan to leave me, but she didn't know what it was. There had been another woman—one other woman. That was eight or nine years earlier, and Nan had never found out.

Mee was no older than Officer Vang when she came to work in my department—back when I was doing marketing for one of those Internet companies that was going to make everyone rich. Her face was lean, cheekbones high and long. She wore gray most days, and the color suited her black hair and dark eyes. She chose tight blouses and short skirts, like all the women on television wore at the time. She looked to me like the opposite of Nan. Where Nan was pink or pale or soft, Mee was brown or dark or firm. I watched her every day, stared at the profile of her body while she microwaved her Lean Cuisines in the break room, and eyed her backside as she hurried back and forth from meeting after meeting. She didn't seem to mind.

Still, it wasn't easy to have an affair. It didn't *just happen*, like people always say. It took work and persistence. I embarrassed myself, changed my mind a hundred times, went to sleep next to Nan full of guilt before I ever laid a hand on Mee.

But when the chance finally came, I felt only thrill while I ran my hands over her unfamiliar body and at last saw the color of her nipples, the faint treasure line below her bellybutton, and the arc of her bare hip. I pulled her against me, groped her, and squeezed her until she finally said, "Easy, Carl. Be easy with me."

When I climbed on top of her, I moved delicately until Mee hooked her legs around me and pulled my body hard against hers. Then there was no more going easy. I was happy, and during those few times we had together, I felt the thing I had once mistaken for love.

Officer Vang's chair was empty when Pete and I came into the lobby after I had bailed him out, helped him collect his belongings, and gotten the details on how he could recover his impounded car in the morning. I stopped and looked at the monitor on Officer Vang's desk, where I could see her shooing a large man in a long coat away from my van. I led Pete across the lobby, and we met Officer Vang in the doorway—her hands balled in front of her chest, jaw clenched, and eyes wet from the cold. She reached out with one fist and slapped my ring of keys into my palm.

She said, "What did I tell you?" and headed inside. I tried to apologize, but she only nodded and kept going.

I followed her back toward her desk, while Pete stood at the door and waited like a small child—rocking from the balls of his feet to his heels, toasty warm inside his puffy down coat, which he wore with a woolen scarf, cap, and gloves.

I leaned on the counter and spoke softly to Officer Vang.

"That's Pete Johnson." I tilted my head in his direction. "We live out in Falcon Heights, just north of the city. You know where that is?"

"I do," she replied.

"I've known Pete for years, and this is the first time he's had any sort of trouble."

Officer Vang craned to see around me and looked Pete up and down.

"Do you know what Pete was in for?" I asked.

"I don't," she said. "They must have told you when—"

"Sure they did. Of course. They picked him up in Frogtown. He had a young woman in his car, a certain type of woman, if you know what I mean."

"I do," she said, and I could tell she was trying not to smile.

I nodded at Officer Vang and gave her a look that said we understood each other. She was putting up a tough front, but I thought she seemed sweet and smart and sly in some way—a little like Mee had been. I hoped she might think well of me, but I realized that when she looked at me she didn't see the person I used to be. She saw thinning hair on top of my head and a messy beard on my chin; she saw the extra inches around my center. She saw a middle-aged man alone in the world.

Behind me, Pete cleared his throat and said, "Ah, Carl. Could we get on our way now?"

His eyes were bloodshot, and the lines beneath them formed dark rings that stretched down near his cheekbones.

"I'm sorry," I said. "I was just checking to see if Officer Vang here has any suggestions regarding who a guy may want to talk to about clearing up this little misunderstanding."

Pete sighed and said, "I'd like to get on home."

I arched my eyebrows and spoke quietly to the officer. "What do you say? Do you have any friends who might get a harmless old man off the hook?"

"I don't. It doesn't work that way," she said. "But if he's a first-timer, he'll just pay a fine for soliciting. No big deal."

A few summers back, Pete and Maryland had celebrated their fortieth wedding anniversary. They'd never had any children, so they threw themselves a backyard party and invited all the neighbors, even the young couples who'd moved to the block only recently and hadn't made much effort to get to know anyone.

Nan volunteered to bring dessert, and she conspired with several other neighbors to surprise Maryland by baking a three-tiered wedding cake—with lemon between the layers of each tier, just like Pete said they'd had at their wedding. Everyone clapped when the women carried the cake outside and set it down on a picnic table. Next to the cake, Nan propped a framed photo from Pete and Maryland's wedding.

When the party was winding down, Nan sliced all but the top tier of the cake and sent pieces home with anyone who would take one. She told Maryland to take the top tier inside, to share it with Pete some other time, and we cleared off the picnic table.

I picked up the photograph and gave it a good long look. In it, Maryland was just a skinny thing. Her face was angular—her cheeks hollow and her chin solid. She wore a wide, open-mouthed smile. Tiny creases marked the corners of her eyes, which were round and bright. *Look at her*, I thought. *Look how beautiful she was.*

Nan said, "Gorgeous, wasn't she?"

I should have agreed—because it was as true as anything—but I made a joke instead.

"Just think," I said. "Now that girl and five of her little friends could camp out in one of Maryland's dresses."

Nan gave a heavy sigh, and I thought I saw tears in her eyes when she turned away.

"What?" I said. "Come on, Nan."

She walked toward the house and didn't look back.

In the van, Pete kept mostly quiet. He thanked me for coming, which he'd already done twice in the jailhouse, and he said he was grateful to have a neighbor he could trust to be discreet, his clever way of asking me to keep my mouth shut.

I wasn't going to tell anybody, but I figured I had a right to know the whole story, which neither Pete nor the cops had taken the time to share. I asked him to spill the beans.

"You know the facts of it," he said.

"Not really. I know what the cops say you did, but I don't know what you thought you were doing, what on earth moved you to go down to Frogtown and pluck yourself a hooker off a street corner."

He only sighed and faced the passenger-side window.

I had taken a different route home, cutting over north of Como Lake and passing through the neighborhood where Nan grew up. She had taken me there when we first started going together because she wanted to introduce me to her parents and show me the streets of her childhood. After we got married, we decided to buy a house nearby so she could be close to home, but her parents sold their place and moved to a new condo on a golf course a few years later.

Pete looked at the passing houses as if he'd never traveled those streets before, and he stayed quiet. Soon we crossed the empty avenue that formed the border between St. Paul and Falcon Heights. I turned onto Simpson and stopped in front of Pete and Maryland's house. He unclipped his seatbelt and thanked me again for helping out.

"Look, Pete, your business is your business. But don't you think you ought to fill me in so I can at least know what secrets I'm keeping?"

He had his fingers on the door latch. He could have gotten right out and walked away if he wanted to, but he sat back and looked me straight in the eye for the first time that night. He pushed his stocking cap off his forehead and smoothed his eyebrows, which had grown long and wild. Since Maryland went to the nursing home, he'd had a general messiness about him—nose and ear hair unchecked, fingernails long and dirty.

"Maybe we can figure a way out of this," I said.

"Honestly," he said. "You know the long and short of it. There isn't much more to tell."

"Just give me the story."

Nan and I screwed for the first time on the floor of her apartment over near the University. We'd been together for a month. It was the dead of summer—a long and hot one—and all we wanted to do was lie around in front of the fan. We played tapes on her roommate's boom box, drank a few cans of Stroh's, and talked all day. I told her everything about myself. I told her which cartoons I'd watched as a kid, how old I was when I tried my first cigarette, why I hated the Beatles, and why at fifteen I'd lied to my friends about losing my virginity. She told me about the old records her father used to play, why she'd been fired from her first part-time job, and how when she was thirteen she had let an older boy put his hand down her pants on the school bus one day.

We stripped off our clothes piece by piece as the afternoon wore into evening and the brick building began to give off a heat of its own. Down to our underwear, we lay on our sides, looked at each other's skin, and rested a hand on each other's hip. We were talked out, and I believed that we had arrived at something, that we had created a connection by sharing our stories, by telling the truth. As if that's all people meant when they talked about falling in love.

When we got out of our underwear and Nan slid herself down onto me, I decided the talk might have meant nothing. I figured love was just a polite name for the kick we got when we put our bodies together, which we did again and again until our sweat soaked the carpet and our backs glowed with red patches of rug-burn.

The truth was, Pete said, Maryland had never gone down on him, and he didn't want to go to his grave without knowing what it felt like.

It was not the sort of thing he'd thought much about over the years, but with his wife in a nursing home and nobody in the house with him, Pete's lonely mind wandered. For some reason—and he didn't know why—he decided that cold and miserable night that he was going to do something about it. He drove to Frogtown, where everybody who has ever drawn a breath in St. Paul knows you can't swing a dead cat without hitting a hooker or a dealer, and he drove up and down each block until he saw a woman alone on a corner. She smiled at him when he slowed near the curb.

"She gets in and says *What do you want, mister? Do you want this? Do you want that? How much you got?* She talks so fast I can hardly keep up," Pete said. "So I gave her an answer, and she told me to pull into this alley and stop the car."

The woman kissed Pete on the cheek and asked for the money up front. He paid—twenty bucks was all—and she unzipped his pants. The moment she slipped her hand into his shorts, a bright light shined on them.

"Then I see men running at the car," Pete said. "I don't know if they are going to kill us both or what in heck they have in mind. Then, lickety-split, they yank us both out of the car, pat us down, lock on the handcuffs, and take us to squad cars."

"They were watching you all along," I said. "You were a sitting duck."

"Sure, and you don't know the half of it."

There was another woman up front in the squad car, sitting on the passenger side. She introduced herself and said she was a reporter from the *Pioneer Press*. She said she wanted to know why men like Pete did what they did.

"No way," I said. "Please tell me you gave her the dementia routine."

"What's that?"

"You know, 'Where am I? Who are you? Wasn't that my niece?'"

"I told her the truth," Pete said, before leaning forward, grabbing the door latch again, and pulling it open. "You see, I was hoping she'd understand—that she'd realize I'm not the kind of person to do something like this."

"You trusted the reporter but didn't want to tell me?" I asked.

He gave me a bashful grin, shook his head, and said, "Good night, Carl."

The truth was, we had a good marriage. We were together five years before our first daughter was born, and we would not have had children at all if we weren't optimistic about the future. We had our second girl two years later, even though the first had tested us in all kinds of ways we never expected. We got along. We pulled each other through. That's all a person can expect in a marriage.

But Nan could never be realistic. She was always putting her nose in another book written by some psychologist she'd heard on the radio or seen on TV. She was always finding new ways to describe our shortcomings as a couple or as a family and new prescriptions for us to lead lives that were more filled with *joy*. That was a big word in those books. *Joy.*

Once I said, "Look around you, Nan. Do you see a world filled with joyful people? Do you see people prancing along and grinning from ear to ear?"

We were in bed, and she had been explaining how we needed to better appreciate the wonders of daily life, to find the joy in common things.

"It's not about how you behave, Carl. It's about how you feel inside." Nan set her book aside, propped herself on one elbow, and clicked off the lamp. "It's about making a genuine life that brings you true happiness."

We lay silently in the dark. I knew she had satisfied herself, that she was pleased she had set me straight again.

"You know something, Nan," I said. "I am happy—not every day, not all the time, but most of the time. I am generally a happy person, and I wish you were, too."

That was the truth. I was happy—with her, with our family, and with our home. I hadn't always done or said the right things, and there were lots of times when I wished hard for something new, something different. But it occurred to me finally that a life with another person could only be so good, that we should expect only so much from another human being. If we can give each other good company and a bit of security, why do we have to ask for more?

That night in the dark, Nan whispered, "I am happy, Carl. I am."

I knew it was a lie, but I didn't say so.

I brought Pete to the impound lot first thing in the morning, left him at the pay booth, and headed straight for the *Pioneer Press* building. When I asked to see the reporter who had been riding around with the cops last night, the young woman at the front desk looked at me like I'd gone out of my head.

Joyless Men

"I'm here for my neighbor," I said. "He's a mixed-up old man. He's not the sort who goes around picking up teenage hookers. He doesn't deserve to have his name all over the newspaper."

The receptionist said she didn't have a clue what I was talking about and she couldn't help me if I didn't have a name. I asked to use her phone and if she wouldn't mind looking up the number of the jail. She dialed the number and handed me the receiver. A deep-voiced man answered, and when I asked for Officer Vang, the girl who worked the front desk, he said she was off duty until the evening, which I should have figured. Neither he nor anybody handy at the jail knew about any reporter being around the night before. I hung up and pleaded with the receptionist to help me out.

"Look," I said, "somebody around here has to be in charge of this reporter, whoever she was. One of the editors must know something about the story."

The woman at the desk frowned, picked up her phone, and turned away from me while she spoke. Five minutes later, a round-faced woman about my age stepped off the elevator and walked straight to the reception desk. She wore a light blue blouse—sleeves rolled to the elbows—and black polyester slacks. She blew curls of faded red bangs off her forehead and smiled. The receptionist introduced her as the city editor.

"So, you're here about the pervert?" She laughed and nodded for me to follow her.

We sat on a bench across the lobby, and I explained everything. I told her every last detail just as Pete had described. But the city editor said the paper was doing a story about the vice squad's crackdown on prostitution and its new approach of targeting the demand—the money-waving, dirty old bastards who come in from the suburbs, scoop up these poor girls, and do terrible things to their young bodies. Part of the police department's plan, she said, was to expose these men, to get their names in the crime reports, to shame the ones who got caught and scare off the others.

"Don't you think every single one of these guys says he deserves a break, that he's never done anything like this before?" she asked.

"Believe me, Pete is a good old soul." I looked her in the eyes, so she would know I wasn't messing with her. "He's mixed up. His wife's got one foot in the grave, and he can't stop wondering if he'll ever know what it feels like, if he'll ever get to experience this thing he's thought about all these years."

"Imagine that," the city editor said, "a lifetime without a hummer."

"Pete's just mixed up. He did a foolish thing."

"Jesus, did he ever. And then he went and told the truth about it."

I couldn't tell if she was making fun of Pete or if she was seeing my side. I didn't know how to make her understand the sadness and trouble her paper could bring to Pete, to Maryland, to all the people in our neighborhood who knew them and wanted only good for them.

"If you could just talk to the reporter," I said. "Just tell her the circumstances."

Two weeks ago, right in time for Christmas, the girls told me about their mother's boyfriend. I had taken them over to the Steak Inn for dinner, and while we waited for the food, my oldest said Mom and Travis had taken them to a Minneapolis hotel with a huge water park. When I asked who Travis was, my youngest said, "Mom's friend."

I excused myself, walked to the hallway near the restrooms, and called Nan on her cell phone. When she answered, I mumbled a hello and struggled over what to say next. She asked if something had gone wrong on the way to the restaurant.

"Travis," I said. "Why do I have to hear about Travis from the girls?"

Joyless Men

She went quiet on the other end of the line.

"Who is he? Where did you meet him?"

"Look, Carl, I have my life now. You have yours. Don't make yourself a victim. I've already heard about your friend with the silver station wagon."

I had to think for a second. "A cleaning lady. The girl with the silver station wagon is a cleaning lady. She comes once a week."

Nan said nothing. I could hear her steady breath. I wondered which neighbors had been gossiping about my cleaning lady. No matter what they'd said, Nan must have seized on it as an excuse, a justification for her actions, a way to make her infidelity look like the direct result of something I had done or failed to do. I knew how that sort of thinking worked.

"If you wanted somebody else," I said, "you should have said so."

I rose early the next morning, dashed out into the cold before sunrise, swiped the newspaper off Pete's step, and scanned it in the light of our foyer. I did the same again the next day and the next. I did it until finally I saw the headline I'd been waiting for: "Vice Cops Target Johns." The story topped the front page of the local news section. I skimmed the text for Pete's name, followed the jump to the inside page, and stopped at this paragraph:

> Officers hear all kinds of excuses from offenders, from the predictable ("I was just giving her a ride") to the bizarre. An older man from suburban Falcon Heights claimed his late wife of four years had steadfastly refused to perform oral sex. He said pure curiosity prompted him to pay for the services he desired, but police interrupted before the transaction could be completed.

That was it—scant details, some of them wrong. I rolled up the paper, snapped its rubber band back in place, and sneaked across to return it to Pete's doorstep. As I retreated down the front walk, I heard the door creak. Then the screen door opened and Linus pattered out at the end of his leash, with Pete trailing behind.

"Good morning, Carl," he said. "Anything good in the paper today?"

I shrugged.

"It's all right," he said. "I've been watching you all week. I appreciate your concern, but I'm not worried about it."

"Oh," I said. "Well, good, you shouldn't be."

Pete nodded and smiled. I waited for Linus and him at the curb. The dog turned and headed up the street, Pete followed, and I fell in beside him. We passed through the entire neighborhood that morning, up and down each block as the sun rose and warmed the air. What a sight we must have made—old Pete with his bushy eyebrows and wild hair poking out from his cap, me with icicles in my beard and flannel pajamas visible between the bottom of my parka and the top of my boots. We walked and walked that day, talking about the weather, our wives, and other things we didn't understand.

Ashes
and
Spit

With one parent recently buried and the other settled in a nursing home, the last thing Trude needed was an old boyfriend coming around, but there he was, standing outside the storm door of her folks' house and looking practically middle-aged now, though still dressed like a kid in baggy shorts and T-shirt. From a sofa in the front room, she watched him look for the doorbell, press the button, and squint into the dimness as one low tone echoed inside. During the seconds before she got up to greet him, she thought: *Here is the first boy I ever loved, the first boy I ever let take off my clothes. Here is the boy who witnessed my cruelest act. Here is someone I wished I'd never see again.*

She walked into the foyer, stopped short of the door, and looked at him, his face mostly lost in shadow and his body framed by the bright August sunshine behind him. Once she was close, he looked down at his feet.

"Hey, Trude," he said. "I heard you were in town."

"Hi, Dan," she replied. "What a surprise."

She moved to let him in, holding open the door as he stepped over the threshold. They were face-to-face for a moment—his still lean and long but the skin dry and toughened now, with reddish patches on his cheekbones and gray rings beneath his eyes, those large, round blue eyes she'd once written childish poems about. She stepped back, and he extended a hand to her. She shook it—his grip warmer and stronger than she expected—and smirked, thinking of the teenage Dan, the boy who was lovably uncomfortable and uncouth.

"What's wrong with you, Dan?" she asked. "You didn't get fat like everyone else."

"You neither," he said.

She tracked his gaze as it moved from her bare feet to her knees, the waistline of her skirt, her chest, her neck. She hoped he wasn't recalling her body—seventeen or eighteen years old and naked. Their eyes met. He looked down again.

He said, "You look exactly the same."

"Yeah, right," she said. "So what's up?"

"I heard you were back," he said. Nodding toward the doorway and street beyond, toward his minivan parked at the curb, he went on, "I thought I'd just come by and see if you were open for lunch."

※※※

Trude bent to kiss her dad, who lay in bed in the late afternoon, a table fan aimed squarely at his chest and a television chattering from the opposite wall. His expression twisted and he rolled his face away.

"For God's sake," he said, his voice croaking and slow-tongued. "Your breath is goddamn awful."

She shushed him and leaned around a half-drawn curtain to see if his roommate was listening or, worse, if his roommate's wife was sitting bedside. She was easily offended and quick to complain to administrators about anything from profane language to violations of the facility's ban on alcohol and tobacco. Trude and her dad had learned that the hard way. Luckily, the roommate was alone and asleep, lips parted to his dark and toothless mouth.

Trude's dad said, "Your breath could knock a buzzard off a shit-wagon."

"Aw, you're sweet," Trude said. She remembered this line from one of the old comedy records he used to play—George Carlin or Steve Martin or somebody from the seventies—and she wasn't bothered. "I'm just happy your olfactory nerves are still firing."

Her dad snorted, which was the only form of laughter he had energy for anymore. "What did you eat?" he asked.

"Let it go, Dad," Trude said, plucking the clipboard from the end of his bed and studying the nurses' notes on his care and condition that day. "I wouldn't pick on you like that, and trust me, I've had opportunities." She slammed the clipboard back into its holder, wheeled around, and stomped out. When she returned, a male nurse followed at her heel, and as she spoke, a deep blush spread from her neck to her cheeks. Through clenched teeth, her voice came out firm and flat.

"You cannot leave him lying there all day," Trude said. "You cannot forget about him."

The nurse, a stocky man whose belly strained the waistband of his baby-blue scrubs, scanned the chart.

"And who are you?" he asked.

"His daughter," she said.

The nurse looked at her, then her father. Trude could see his mind at work, trying to match the German man and the Korean woman.

"I'll have him in the chair in a minute," the nurse said, walking to retrieve the Hoyer lift from the corner. "Maybe you can take him outside for some fresh air."

"You understand his history with bedsores, don't you?" Trude asked. "You understand that he can't be left here to rot? He has to be moved regularly, and he has to spend time in his chair every day."

It Takes You Over

With the lift in place over the bed, the nurse paused to slide open the top drawer of the nightstand. He pulled out a baby bottle—its nipple stained a golden brown—and held it out for Trude.

"I believe this may have come from you," the nurse said, leveling his heavy-lidded gaze in her direction. "And I believe your father is familiar with our alcohol policy."

Trude nodded as her father snorted again.

The nurse waved her away and said, "I'll have him ready in a minute."

After retreating to the hallway, Trude cupped a hand over her mouth and exhaled. The garlic blast brought water to her eyes. She hadn't wanted to tell her dad about the lunch with Dan, hadn't felt like going over it again.

Dan had insisted on taking her to the new Olive Garden in town, which he explained had the only decent Italian food within ninety miles. Trude knew what he meant. Minneapolis stood an hour and a half to the north. They waited thirty minutes to get a table and looked at menus while they sat in the lobby. They were famished and ready to order the moment their waitress arrived. Both asked for fettuccine alfredo.

While they waited for the food, Trude inquired about old classmates. She was out of the loop—way out of it. After splitting with Dan halfway through their first year away at separate colleges, she had avoided the high school crowd whenever she came home to Mankato. Dan, on the other hand, had returned after five years in school, married a local girl he met at the office, and dug in. He could answer Trude's questions about what had become of classmates—all but one.

"Tanya Schmitz?" he asked. "You're not still thinking about that are you?"

"Only when I'm in this town," Trude said. "Another reason I haven't gone to the reunions."

"When did that happen?" he said, sipping diet cola through a straw. "Eighth grade?"

She nodded.

"And you beat yourself up about it all through high school," he went on, "and here we are, fifteen years after graduation, and you're still thinking about it."

"Eighteen years," she said. "And I'm only asking what happened to Tanya. I don't think about it much. Honestly, I don't. It's just this town. When I'm back here it's like my brain clicks through a slideshow of bad memories."

"And that's one of them?"

"It's not always the first one, but it's in the carousel."

"Hmm," Dan said. "Well, if I tell you she's rich and happy and has a perfect little family, will you forget about it?"

"That would probably do the trick," Trude said. A thin smile spread on her face, which she cocked to the side, and she leaned forward. "Please say it's true."

Dan shook his head, and as he did, Trude replayed the scene in her mind. Tanya Schmitz had always sat alone among the last five kids on the afternoon bus—with Dan and Trude and a couple of sixth-graders they all ignored. Tanya was a chunk, a redhead with a bad perm, puffy cheeks, and thick lips. While her expression seemed frozen in smugness, she was actually a timid sort, the kind of kid who never looked prettier girls in the eye. For some reason, mostly because Tanya was such a safe target, Trude couldn't help but razz her.

"Hey, Red," Trude said one day when Tanya rose as the bus came to her stop. "Lay off the Twinkies tonight, okay?"

At fourteen, Trude operated on the edge of her school's circle of cool people. She had adopted a pseudo-punker look, her black hair marred by one broad stripe of pink dye and knotted with one of her mother's old scarves, and she thought of herself as an eighth-grade version of a neutral country, neither in nor out. But Tanya was on nearly everybody's list of outsiders.

Pulling on her backpack as the bus rattled to a halt, she glared at Trude. "Shut up," Tanya said, voice quivering. She was quiet for a moment, her lips shaking, before she added, "Why don't you lay off the egg rolls?"

As the younger kids snickered, Trude felt the wind go out of her. She had just been faced by the lowest of the low. She had to act.

"Hey, Tanya!" she said, jumping up from her seat and stepping into the aisle. When Tanya ignored her and strode toward the front of the bus, Trude hawked a ball of phlegm and saliva into her mouth, making a noise that got the other girl's attention.

Tanya whirled and said, "Don't you dare."

Trude pursed her lips and spat just as Tanya screamed, "No!" The yellow wad streamed directly into Tanya's mouth and splattered against her coiled tongue. Tanya swatted at her lips, oozing Trude's spit and her own as she ran sobbing from the bus.

Now, all these years later, Trude still felt weak when she thought of it.

"You know why I did it?" she asked Dan.

"She smarted off," he said.

"Yeah, right. But spitting in someone's face? Into someone's mouth? Where did that come from?" Trude asked. "I thought I was a nice person, you know? Not like that, not someone who would even think of such a thing."

"Kids do mean stuff," Dan said. "If that's the worst you've ever done to someone, you're not so bad."

"No," she said. "I spat into her mouth. Think about that."

As she spoke, Trude raised a finger to her lips, then zipped it along a quick line toward Dan's. "My spit went into her mouth," she said.

"I know," he said.

"What's worse than that?" Trude asked. "Wouldn't you rather get punched or slapped? Wouldn't you rather someone knock you down or kick you in the crotch or even smash an egg on your head? I would."

Dan shrugged, and the waitress arrived with their food. He said, "I honestly don't know what happened to Tanya. Moved away, I think. Let's change the subject."

"Okay," Trude replied. She shook her head and smoothed her napkin over her lap. "Tell me about your divorce."

Trude wheeled her dad onto the patio behind Sibley Manor, which squatted in an old part of town near the Minnesota River, and dragged a lawn chair over to be at his side. She pulled a five-pack of cigars out of her purse and unwrapped one.

"Haven't had time to get some good ones?" her dad asked.

"Sorry, I meant to," she said. "Maybe I'll ask Dan to pick some up for you."

"Who?"

"Dan Beal," she said. "He stopped by the house."

Her dad reached out his right hand, his good one, the one he could still control well enough to hold a smoke or a drink. He held the cigar—a stubby Swisher—between his thumb and forefinger and brought it to his lips, which he puckered the way a young child would to drink from a garden hose. Trude flicked the lighter and held it up while her dad drew long, slow breaths that brought orange to the tip of the cigar.

"Who's that?" her dad said, coughing out his words along with a mouthful of smoke.

"*Dan Beal*," Trude repeated. "From high school? He was my boyfriend? You liked him? You said I never should have broken up with him?"

Her dad sat with his right elbow propped on the armrest and kept the cigar always near his face. Seven years had passed since he gave up the walker and went into the wheelchair, four years since he lost control of the digits on his left hand. He coughed again, harder this time, and Trude heard the muck in his airways, which he could never seem to clear away, no matter how hard he hacked or cleared his throat. He took another pull from his cigar.

"Your mother said that," he said. "I would never get involved in that sort of thing."

Trude snorted. "Okay, Mom said that you said that I never should have broken up with him."

Her dad smirked and nodded. Then he said, "What'll we do without your mother?"

Trude didn't know what to say. Her family had always functioned under certain assumptions—her father's disease would continue its slow destruction, her mother would outlive him, his death might finally come as a relief to them both after thirty-odd years on their way to an inevitable conclusion. Then, six weeks earlier, Trude's mother had had a heart attack while scrubbing the bathtub and died alone on the bathroom floor.

Since the burial, Trude had shuttled back and forth between Mankato and St. Joseph, a tiny town a couple hours away where she worked in admissions at a Catholic women's college, her alma mater. She was testing the patience of her supervisors and running herself out of energy. And still her parents' home bulged with things to pack away in storage, sell off, or throw out. And the house itself had to be cared for until she could sell the place and see that the money was set aside for her dad. Trude didn't want to trouble him with these problems—all the work and hard decisions ahead—so she kept quiet awhile.

"It stinks out here," she finally said.

Her dad nodded. "The river. It's low by this time of summer. Dirty. Muddy."

"Smells like dead fish," Trude said, staring at the row of cottonwoods lining the river, which was obscured by a flood-control berm rising beyond the fence at the back of the nursing home property. "Hey, I've got something else for you."

She reached into her purse and drew out a baby bottle half-filled with brown liquid.

"Brandy?" her dad asked.

"Uh-huh." She always brought brandy.

"One sip," he said. "Then you keep it until I'm in bed. We'll hide it under the covers. I don't want that fat-load nurse to take it away again."

Trude returned to Mankato early the next Saturday and got to work around the house. She mowed the grass and ripped weeds from the flowerbeds, then went inside to continue sorting through the mix of worthless junk and family heirlooms her mother had accumulated in the basement. Trude had picked away at the task during each of her weekend visits, yet she believed the end might never come.

She sat on a broken-down dehumidifier and surveyed the room, cluttered with half-filled boxes and bloated garbage bags. She wondered if anyone would care if she got rid of everything and what would happen if she didn't. Would the things she boxed up and kept for herself today only be waiting for someone else to sort through once she was dead? Who would be there to sort her things anyway?

When the doorbell rang, she knew it would be Dan. He stood outside the screen door, a cigar box tucked under one arm. He wore baggy shorts again, with a loose T-shirt and some old sneakers. Trude could not figure out why guys of Dan's age insisted on walking around with their shirts untucked, but she had to admit to herself that she was happy to see him.

"Come on in," she said. "Thanks for getting the cigars."

"They're Dominican," he said, looking pleased with himself as he pulled the door closed, "but the guy at the smoke shop said they were grown from Cuban seeds."

"And you believed that?" Trude asked. "How sweet you are."

He laughed and denied that he'd been suckered; she shook her head and waved for him to follow her to the basement. At the foot of the stairs, she paused, and he stood beside her, his shoulder touching hers.

"I didn't know your mother was a packrat," he said. "She seemed so organized."

"She was—back in the day," Trude said. "But the sicker he got, the less she kept on top of things. I've found boxes full of canceled checks from the mid-nineties, years worth of cooking magazines, mail for my dad that she never even opened. Things got away from her. She probably planned to catch up once Dad was in the nursing home, but then, you know, she had to go and die."

Dan put his hand on her back, right at the base of her neck, and rested it there a moment.

"Well, let's do it," he said—proceeding to spend the rest of the day hauling away things as fast as Trude could load boxes and tape them closed. He filled his minivan and ferried back and forth to the Salvation Army, the local dump, and the storage place without a break. He worked and kept on working.

Trude got rid of everything she could part with in good conscience. When she found a box of her own baby clothes, she set aside the lime-colored outfit she'd been wearing on the flight from Korea, along with her baptismal gown and a fuzzy sleeper that was too cute to toss out. On a dusty shelf, she found a framed photo of her and Dan at the prom. Her mother had kept it piled among old family pictures. Dan wore a white tux with royal blue bowtie and cummerbund. At seventeen, he was six feet tall and rail thin with a haircut that made him look like he was ready for boot camp. Back then, she'd wondered how he escaped the notice of the other girls. Now she understood.

"What you got there?" Dan asked after he bounded down the stairs. She handed him the frame, and he looked it over and whistled. "Look at you. I'd forgotten about that dye job—and the eye makeup."

The girl in the photo seemed like a long lost friend to Trude. She wore a black dress—strapless and snug, exploiting what little cleavage she had—and she had bleached yellow streaks in her hair, which was cut in a severe line at chin-length. Trude wondered how she'd had that much nerve.

"I made that dress," she said.

"I know," Dan replied, then nudged her with his elbow. "Remember how pissed you were when I practically tore out the zipper trying to get you out of that little number?"

Trude looked at him, supposing she should be troubled that he so readily recalled such a thing. The prom was half of her lifetime ago. Everything with Dan was at least half of her lifetime ago.

"Here." She handed him the frame. "I'd like you to have it."

When she brought one of the Dominican cigars over to her dad, she found him in his chair and waiting.

"Good, you're here," he said. "There's an empty bottle in the drawer."

"Hello to you, too." She removed the baby bottle from the bedside drawer and, after checking around to make sure neither a nurse nor the roommate's wife was watching, replaced it with a fresh one.

Outside, she lit the cigar and watched her dad exhale a long, satisfied stream of smoke. He took another puff and inhaled deeply.

"Those things will get you an early grave," she said.

"Funny," he croaked.

The midday sun shined against her dad's pale, grayish skin. He slumped to the left in his wheelchair, his midsection crumpled. He wore a cardigan sweater over a hospital gown, his bare feet purple and swollen, yellow toenails flaking off.

When Trude got behind his chair, reached under his armpits, and tried to straighten him, the ash from his cigar dropped onto his thigh. She brushed it away.

"Forget it," he said. Once she'd sat back down, he asked, "Been seeing that old boyfriend?"

"He's helping me out."

"Good. Maybe we'll get you married off yet." His voice was stronger than usual, sloppy still but loud and steady. "That'd please your mother."

Trude didn't know if she should laugh or cry. She turned away and stared at the trees along the river, their leaves silvery in the summer light.

"She didn't want you to be lonely," he said.

"I'm not," she said.

"You were never supposed to be an only child, you know. She wanted three, at least."

"I know."

"She planned to name one after each of her closest friends."

"I know." Trude turned and glared at her dad.

"Susan, Marie, and Gertrude."

"Dad," Trude said, "I know this. I know, I know, I know. And I know the disease wrecked everything. I know. Why rehash it?"

They sat silent, and he chewed the tip of his cigar between puffs. He made a small, approving sigh after each release of smoke.

"Why the hell didn't you start with *Susan?*" she asked. "Hard enough being the only Korean in a roomful of little Germans and Swedes, but then I had to deal with that albatross of a name."

"It's lovely," he said, his lopsided grin returning. "I don't know what you're complaining about."

Trude invited Dan for dinner the following Sunday and planned to get in her car for the drive back to St. Joseph as soon as they were through. She hoped he would agree to deal with the realtor, get the house on the market, hang on to some keys in case anybody wanted to see it, and generally keep an eye on things so she could stay home for a couple of weeks and catch up on her own life. Having worked his way into a good job at one of the local banks, Dan knew whom to call and how to get things done in this town. Trude trusted him.

She baked a tin of lasagna she'd discovered in the freezer downstairs, and they washed it down with the bottles of Schell's that he brought along. Trude's weary body ached, and her head felt light after only a couple beers.

"So," she said, as they sat over smeared plates and wadded napkins in her mother's kitchen, "why don't you tell me about the worst thing you've ever done to another person?"

"What?" Dan said, shaking his head. "No way."

"You know my secrets," she said. "You've seen me at my worst. You were there for the Tanya Schmitz thing. You know exactly when and where I lost my virginity. You watched me drink lime vodka until I puked through my nose. And so on and so on."

Dan smiled, but Trude continued. "You knew all of my dark secrets back in school, but you never did anything as bad." She stood and gathered a stack of dishes—mismatched pieces of Corelle her mother had gathered from garage sales and grocery-store giveaways. They were nearly unbreakable, perfect for the household with someone whose dexterity was in steady, inevitable decline. As she carried them to the sink, Trude said, "You were always an innocent bystander."

"Except for the virginity deal."

"Yeah, right." Trude nodded and laughed a little.

The dishes scraped into the empty sink before she dropped in the stopper and cranked on the hot water. The legs of Dan's chair chattered on the floor as he turned toward her. She grabbed the half-eaten tin of lasagna from the stovetop, tossed it in the garbage pail, and squirted dish soap into the sink. Then only the splashing of water and chafing of dish against dish interrupted the silence.

"Okay," Dan said. "Here it is, in brief."

Towel slung over her shoulder, Trude shut off the tap and leaned against the lip of the countertop. She looked Dan in the eyes. He looked away as he began his story.

"I had this girlfriend," he said. "This was in college. I was a junior. She was a sophomore. We met in an econ class. We just went crazy for each other, you know? Like only people who are that young can do? A total infatuation, I guess, but at the time, it felt real."

He cleared his throat and fiddled with the label on his bottle of beer, his face blushing but expressionless.

"We were absolutely glued to each other—always together, all over each other, baby talk, holding hands, public displays like nobody's business." He chuckled and glanced up at Trude. "Not my style, as you know."

She nodded.

"In hindsight, I know it probably wasn't real, but at the time, I just friggin' loved her. I was in deep—way, way deep." He paused. "And then one day I read her diary."

"Really?" Trude asked. "How'd you get your hands on it?"

"It was always around," he said. "It was just one of those notebooks, you know, a blank book, no lock or anything. I was in her room watching TV while she went off to class, and I picked it up without really thinking. I just flipped it open and started reading.

"And I've got to tell you that ninety-nine percent of what she wrote there was sweet and true and completely innocent. But there were some things—little references to her high-school boyfriend and some stupid daydreams she'd had about him. It said something like 'What if he was Mr. Right and I didn't know it?' Then it said she loved me but worried we were moving too fast."

He paused again, shook his head, and added, "That crushed me, just killed me. I thought we were totally perfect together, no doubts. She had these other ideas, and I couldn't bear it."

He sipped from his beer.

"What did you do?"

"I waited two or three days, and then I dumped her," he said. "I called her up on the phone and said we were done, and when she asked why, I said, 'You know why.'"

Dan cleared his throat and went on. "And then she freaked out. She sobbed and sobbed. She wouldn't accept it. She kept saying, 'Why? Why? Why?' She kept calling me, coming to my apartment, sending me letters. Christ, even her mother sent me a letter. And I would not take her back, and I would not say why. Never."

The room went silent. Trude inhaled the reek of garlic and burnt red sauce and thought how good the house smelled when her mother would make dinner, how her mother would never have dreamed of serving frozen food to a guest, back when her life was under control. She looked at Dan, glum and silent now, and wished she hadn't asked the question. She said she was sorry.

"It's okay," he said. "Now you know what eats at me. So we're square."

Earlier that day, Trude's visit with her dad had been brief. A rain shower had blown over, but water pooled on the seats of the patio chairs at Sibley Manor, forcing her to stand alongside his wheelchair while he had a cigar. He smoked more quickly than ordinary and had little to say, as if he sensed she wanted to get going.

"I forgot to bring a bottle," she said.

He only nodded.

"I'll try to drop one by later," she said. "But I've got some things to do—Dan's coming for dinner—and I need to get on the road at a reasonable hour."

"Big date, huh?" he asked, his voice tired that day.

Trude rolled her eyes.

"Remind me," he said. "Why did you break up with that kid anyway?"

"Good Lord," she said. "We were eighteen, going to school 300 miles apart. What was the sense of that?"

"I suppose," he said.

Trude sighed, relieved her dad had accepted her answer, but she couldn't help thinking about what had gone wrong back then.

The trouble started at the end of Thanksgiving break during her freshman year. Packed and ready to return to St. Joseph—with her mother gone shopping and her father stuck behind his walker and largely confined to the ground floor—Trude had felt free to indulge Dan's request for a goodbye quick one up in her bedroom. In the swift way of beginners, they were naked and entwined on the floor, their thin bodies seeming to fit together like strands of rope.

After he finished, Dan wheezed and laughed, laying his head on her chest, the room quiet once they'd caught their breath. She heard her father then, calling her name from somewhere downstairs, bellowing again and again "Truuuude." She dressed and ran to find him, fallen to the kitchen floor, his walker toppled on its side, his body lacking strength to raise itself. When she grabbed his hand and pulled, he said, "Damn it, kid, what are you doing up there?"

Dan had followed Trude downstairs, and when he asked "Is everything okay?" she looked at him in the kitchen doorway, his sweatshirt inside out and the fly on his jeans zipped only halfway. She hoped her father wouldn't notice, but he was staring straight at her boyfriend and looking pissed.

By Christmas that year, she and Dan were finished. All this time later, she didn't feel like explaining it to her dad, to Dan, to anyone.

"Ancient history," she said quietly, talking mainly to herself. "No use rehashing it."

Her dad nodded again and said, "I wish you'd brought the brandy."

After the plates were dried and put away, Trude suggested they drink the last two beers from Dan's six-pack on the front steps. He offered to haul the kitchen garbage out to the can and asked if he could try one of the Dominicans he'd picked up for her dad. The gray of twilight was giving way to darkness by the time they got outside. Trude had switched off the front light so the moths wouldn't bounce around and bother them. She handed Dan a cigar, some matches, and a cutter she dug out of the junk drawer.

"Do you know how to handle this?" she asked.

"Don't worry," he said. "I've been around a little bit."

He cut one end and lit it, inhaling deep into his chest and releasing sweet-smelling smoke through his nose and mouth. They talked and sipped their last bottles of Schell's while he continued with the cigar. Thoughts of the future—how much she might net from the house sale, how she might protect some money from the IRS and the nursing home, where she might stay when she returned to visit her dad—occupied their conversation. When they'd finished the beers, she retrieved two sodas from the fridge so they could stay there on the steps and talk some more. Dan smoked the cigar down to a nub so small that he singed his fingers while taking a last, long draw. He dropped the piece onto the concrete and shook his hand.

"Are you trying to get sick or what?" Trude asked.

Dan scrunched his brow.

"I've never seen anyone smoke that much of a cigar in one sitting," she said.

"Really?" He picked up the glowing stub and let it fall into the shallow bit of beer left in the bottom of his bottle. "How else are you gonna smoke it?"

"It's not like a giant cigarette." She figured he'd kept on smoking it because he didn't want their evening to end. She leaned and nudged him with her shoulder. "Even my dad only smokes them halfway."

Dan bent over and kissed Trude's cheek. She twisted toward him and kissed him square on the mouth—his lips dry against hers and his tongue, which tasted of Dominican weeds, moving in a way she dimly recalled. They stopped, looked at each other, and turned to face the empty street.

"Whew," she said.

"Yeah," he said, "that was nice."

She wanted to say, "Sure, but your breath could knock a buzzard off a shit-wagon," but she only patted his leg and nodded.

Trude knew that if she left right then, she wouldn't be home until well after midnight and the three beers would make her drowsy on the road. She also knew that if she didn't report for work on time tomorrow, she might exhaust her employers' last bits of sympathy. She glanced at Dan, his face aglow like that of a boy with a new crush, and he smiled at her. Before she leaned to kiss him again, she thought: *Here is the home I thought would always await me, the place where my parents tried to make a family while their lives crumbled. And here is a person I don't want to leave behind again.*

The Baroness

Any beauty Kayla had was in her face—a pale and perfect oval marked by dark eyes, black curls falling on her forehead. A lot could be said for that face, but her body seemed unfinished. When we stood together, I could slide my hands across her back, over the hardness of her hips, up to her ribs and chest, and all the time they would just glide and glide. What I felt was an absence of shape, a lack of interruption on a vertical drop from shoulders to ankles. Still, she had that face and those curls, and she moved quickly and clumsily when her clothes came off, as if she couldn't stand to wait any longer.

I shared an apartment with a roommate back then. It was a shit time for our kind of guy. We'd come out of college into a world that had no appetite for us, and we had to take whatever work we could find. We were temps and tellers, computer salesmen and customer service reps. My roommate had a good temp job at the State Capitol and a girlfriend of his own. She had her own apartment, which meant he mostly used our place for storage, a happy thing for me.

It Takes You Over

I brought Kayla home after a movie and six or seven vodka sours on the patio at Sweeney's bar. We stumbled in, laughing and nervous, and she went into the bathroom while I mixed plastic-bottle rum into two glasses of Coke. "We deserve a nightcap," she'd said before the bathroom door clicked. From the kitchen I heard the toilet flush, the door open, and her footsteps to the living room. I called for her to meet me on the couch, and when she didn't answer, I leaned around the corner. She stood in the center of the room, her clothes gone, her body pale and smooth as a sheet of aluminum. There was nothing really to look at, nothing but some dark wisps here, pink circles there. In the dim light, she clasped her hands over her belly and said, "Everything okay?"

I left the drinks on the counter and led her to the couch, where she pulled me down onto her before I could untuck, unbutton, or unzip. She kissed with her lips wide apart and her tongue sopping my mouth, chin, neck. She kept silent, other than the slopping and smacking of her ridiculous kisses. I couldn't kiss her back like that, so I just let my mouth fall open. When I laughed, she licked my teeth. When I turned away, she slurped my earlobe. Kissing Kayla felt embarrassing and crazy, but it was fun. I'd never associated fun with kissing, which I realized right then, with her licking the roof of my mouth. And when the kisses slowed, she pushed down on my shoulders. I tried to hold still, but she kept pushing me downward. I kissed the hard plate at the center of her chest, and she pushed against my shoulders. I kissed the firm plane around her bellybutton, and she pushed down.

I thought, *How can I do this? I hardly know you.* But I didn't stop her. I closed my eyes and moved lower, thinking of her sloppy kisses and trying not to laugh. She tightened her legs around me, held me there. She never said a word, never made a sound other than soft, short breaths. I only knew to stop when the rigid metal of her body turned to something molten. She let her legs fall open. And there I was, kneeling on the floor, all my clothes on, like I'd hardly been involved.

The Baroness

A couple years after finishing college, I met Kayla at a breakfast-and-lunch dive near the office where I was temping. She studied design at a little art college on Summit Avenue and earned extra cash by waiting tables, not because she was broke, but because her father required her to have a job. She usually took my order if I sat at the counter, which I almost always did because I almost always went to lunch alone. Sometimes she stood near me during idle seconds, leaning against the counter and telling me about herself.

I wanted to believe she'd taken a real interest, that she'd not found my company merely a tolerable way to kill time. I'd been only marginally successful with the girls at my college, and now I went around every day feeling like a dope, with my light blue shirts and striped ties, my tidy haircut and neatly trimmed sideburns. I'd never had luck with a girl like Kayla, a skinny art student who wore a black T-shirt to work every day, who rolled her sleeves up onto her shoulders, who used a red bandana to hold back her long hair, who looked a little too cool for the room.

I spent a lot of money on grilled cheese sandwiches and fries. I took lunch early or went late so she wouldn't be rushed the whole time. I kept a mental list of things I liked about her: how she spoke too loudly sometimes, how she laughed easily, how her eyebrows showed her emotion, how they rarely sat still. I saw the beauty in her face, and I didn't get tired of it.

Working up nerve to finally ask her out, I stalled at the register as she rang me up. I stared at the candy under the glass of the countertop—the Wrigley's gum and Velamints, the Life Savers and Snickers bars. "Maybe I should get some Big Red," I said. Kayla laughed and replied, "All that stuff is ancient. You don't want it."

It Takes You Over

I hoped my roommate, Nate, could get me a job at the Capitol. He'd been a temp there for two legislative sessions and, I supposed, must have accumulated a little pull with somebody somewhere. But when I went to visit him at work we spent the whole time talking about Kayla. I explained her preferences and the persistent way she imposed them.

"Well," he said, "you're a regular Orel Hershiser."

"That's pretty weak," I replied. We were in the cafeteria of the State Office Building. The place was dead because the Legislature was in recess. The cheeseburgers and fries tasted like they'd been cooked in a microwave. "Anyway, I don't know why I'm telling you this."

"Oh, relax," he said. "Consider it off the record."

"I guess it's not my favorite thing."

"So don't do it."

"Not an option." I hesitated to say much more. "With her, it's important."

I expected him to laugh. He only chewed his food and stared thoughtfully toward a distant point on the ceiling. After two bites of burger and a fistful of fries, he rocked forward.

"I can't believe I have to explain this," he said.

"What?" I leaned forward, too.

"Don't be a jackass," he whispered. "It's a good thing, and you're lucky to be there. So shut up. Quit being an idiot. Forget all that teenage bullshit about tacos and tuna fish, if that's your problem."

He paused and glanced around. We both laughed.

"Seriously, just put your mind on something sweet," he continued, no longer quiet. "Think of candy. It's Juicy Fruit. It's a pineapple Life Saver. It's lemon-lime Bubblicious."

Kayla's dad was one of those guys who wore funny T-shirts. He had one with a little pocket on the chest. The words "A day with the kids" were stitched on the pocket, and above it was a burst of embroidery forming a bundle of twenty-dollar bills. He had another one that said "I brake for lutefisk suppers." I'd never tried a single bite of lutefisk, but I'd heard the old joke: There are only two things that taste like lutefisk, and one of them is lutefisk.

"What does your father do?" he'd asked the first time we met. "Where'd you grow up?"

"He's done a lot of things," I said. We stood in his kitchen—Kayla and her parents and me—and leaned against the counters. "I grew up in St. Paul, out by Como Park."

Her dad was one of those guys who thought he could instantly size you up, could ask a couple questions and have you pegged. He said, "What's that mean—*he's done a lot of things?* What kind of things?"

"Just kidding," I said. Kayla watched me, and I knew she was nervous I'd say the wrong thing. "My dad moved to Sioux Falls. I guess he's selling real estate now."

"Divorced?" he asked.

I nodded, and he shrugged, waved a hand, and told me to come downstairs so he could show me something.

"You're on your own," Kayla said.

Her dad was also one of those guys with a game room in the basement, a nice one with a pool table, dartboard, and old-school pinball machine. He seemed proud; none of it looked like it got used much. And he wanted to play pool, even though I told him I hadn't done it often and wasn't any good. He racked the balls, laughed at my break, and started knocking them in with ease.

"What kind of work do you do?" I asked, trying to seem cool, like I didn't care that he was killing me and that I looked like a pansy with a pool cue in my hands.

"Insurance," he said, leaning over and lining up the shot. He snapped it off, and there were two cracks—the cue ball against his target, the target against the back of the pocket. "I run the company's fraud investigations office in Minneapolis."

I could tell he thought this was some big stuff. He moved slowly around the table, examining the situation, crouching to eye potential shots. He didn't look at me when he talked, couldn't be distracted by our conversation. He paced and made a show of how well he understood the game.

"You like that?" I asked.

"Huh?" he said, finally glancing at me, an annoyed look on his face. "Do I like what?"

"Insurance," I said.

He didn't bother to answer.

After he'd destroyed me in two games and racked up a third, Kayla came down the stairs with three bottles of Heineken. Her dad was one of those guys who drank Heineken, who seemed to think it showed class, even though it tasted skunky and cost too much. He was pleased she'd brought the beers.

"Maybe you ought play this game, Kay," he said. "Minnesota Fats over there is having an off day."

They both laughed, but I didn't give a damn. I slid onto one of the stools he kept lined against the wall, sipped his shit beer, and imagined the things I'd done with his daughter. Things I'd done just an hour or so before we came over. Places my hands had been. Places my mouth had been. And when Kayla leaned to take a shot, I dreamed that someday I would get his daughter into this room and I would strip her, bend her over that pool table, have a go that way, or maybe we'd climb right up on it and let our sweat soak into the green felt. We would do that. Someday. I felt sure.

Only twelve-year-olds chewed Bubblicious, and Juicy Fruit made my teeth hurt. I bought a few rolls of Life Savers—the standard-issue pack of five flavors. They put in too many cherries, and those tasted like cough drops. There were fewer oranges and lemons and limes. I liked the limes. If I got lucky I'd

The Baroness

find three pineapples in a whole pack. The pineapples were my favorite. I'd forgotten what they tasted like. They were sweet, but not too sweet. Tart, but not too tart.

I killed almost two years temping for Great River Software, my first job after graduating college. Lots of guys like me were temps back then, temps for years, temps forever. All that meant was they didn't have to give us health insurance and they could shitcan us whenever they felt like it. But what could I do? I had no skills. I had no experience. I had no value, no leverage, no cause for optimism.

Part of my job was to drive all over hell on those never-ending two-lane highways of outstate Minnesota and teach people how to use some software Great River developed for the state's labor department. Sometimes Kayla skipped classes, called in sick, and rode along with me. Those were the happy days.

Once I brought her along on a three-meeting swing through Red Wing, Winona, and Rochester. In each city, I would meet with staff at the job center and explain how we were converting to an Internet-based system, how job seekers would upload their résumés, and employers would be able to match their needs with the qualifications of a statewide pool of candidates. Most times I had to explain what *upload* meant. Sometimes I had to explain what the Internet was. *Oh,* the local bureaucrats would say, *so this is the information superhighway, so this is the World Wide Web, so this is the infobahn, so this is cyberspace.* I'd say, *Yes, it's all the same thing.* None of us really knew what we were doing.

"I've got a great idea," I said, as we zipped along Highway 61 at sunrise, heading for an eight o'clock in Red Wing.

"What?" Kayla wore a pair of Bermuda shorts and a plaid golf shirt she'd found at a thrift store. She always spoke proudly of her second-hand finds. That's what rich girls did in those days. She had one long, thin leg raised and bent, the sole of her Birkie smudging the dashboard. With her hair pushed behind her ears and not a speck of makeup on her face, she looked perfect to me. "Let's hear this brilliant idea."

"You'll need an open mind," I said.

"Yeah?"

"It'll make our day lots more fun."

"Okay," she said. "Out with it."

So I pitched a proposal: We would commit an act of public carnality in each of the towns we had to visit that day. I could hurry my meetings a bit, but still we would need to be quick. We would find a park or a parking lot or any other place that seemed right.

"So we're becoming exhibitionists, are we?"

"No, that's not it," I said. "We have to get away with it."

"Okay," she said. "But I've got a couple ground rules for you."

"Fine." I tried to play cool, but I was getting all charged up like a thirteen-year-old. "Anything you say."

"Rule number one: We cannot do it in this car."

"Agreed." We were riding in a Chevrolet Corsica from the state motor pool. "That would be smart."

"Rule number two: You have to fully commit to this."

"Huh?" I squeezed the steering wheel. "What does that mean?"

"You don't get to just unzip and wriggle your pants down a few inches." Kayla smiled.

"I think that's how it works," I said, but I knew what she was telling me. I knew what she expected.

"Fully commit," she said. "That's the only way."

In Red Wing, we criss-crossed town desperately after my meeting, knowing we had maybe twenty minutes before we'd need to get back onto the road and head for Winona. We ended up in the women's bathroom at a riverside park, where we crowded into a stall, pulled off a few things, and got to work. Kayla pressed her back against one wall, raised one leg, propped her foot on the toilet paper dispenser, and pushed me down by the shoulders. I knelt on the concrete floor and complied, feeling the grit of sand and chipped paint through the knees of my chinos. The flavor of pineapple Life Savers flooded my mouth, and I thought I'd never get tired of it. When Kayla's quick gasps gave way to a long, slow breath, she pulled me up and said "Hurry!"

She unzipped my pants, and I worked them down. She kept a foot on the toilet paper dispenser and her back against the wall. I hurried, and no one else came into the bathroom the whole time. When we ran out laughing, we surprised an old woman who was stooped outside the small building, looping her collie's leash around the drainpipe of the drinking fountain.

"What's the matter here?" she said, indignant.

"Nothing," I said.

Never slowing down, Kayla grabbed my hand and smiled at the old lady. "I got carsick. He was just making sure I was okay."

I barely made the Winona meeting on time and had to floor it to get to Rochester for the day's last session, which went exactly like all the others. Our plan had fallen apart after one stop, but we didn't care. Kayla and I wore goofball smiles all day—the smiles of people who've gotten away with something, who've stolen a bit of candy from the 7-11. We held hands as we sped along two-lane highways and passed through quiet little towns she said she'd never heard of. On the way back to St. Paul, I stopped at a DQ and bought us an enormous Mister Misty to share. She wanted cherry, and I went along. Like a couple of dopes, we got two spoons and laughed at ourselves as we fed each other heaping mouthfuls.

I started keeping a five-flavors roll in my pocket all the time. It became my thing. I'd never had a thing, but I'd noticed that lots of men—grown-up men I'd known—had a thing. My

It Takes You Over

grandpa always kept a toothpick in his chest pocket. My father kept Doublemint gum in the ashtray of his car. Even Kayla's dad had his Heineken. So every morning I slipped a roll of Life Savers into my pants pocket—always the left front pocket—and went out into the world. I shared them with friends and coworkers, but if a pale-yellow one showed on top, I popped it into my mouth. I never shared the pineapples.

Kayla's dad liked backing people into impossible positions. He always had questions, and he behaved as if the universe entitled him to ask anything he pleased. He came after me pretty good during a trip to a cabin he'd rented way the hell up on Lake Bemidji. Six of us made the trip—Kayla, her parents, her little sister, her little sister's friend, and me. The cabin had three bedrooms.

"You can throw your bag in Kayla's room," he told me when we arrived. "Then you'll flop on the couch at night."

Kayla and I expected as much; her mother had warned us. Still, she protested. After we'd unloaded all the stuff, she said, "There are twin beds in there, Dad. Don't worry about it."

A huge sectional sofa dominated the cabin's living room, and Kayla's dad had settled in at the crux of its two sides. Legs crossed and hands behind his head, he posed there like the picture of Northwoods ease. He stared through the large front window at the blue-black water of the lake, and he didn't flinch when his daughter suggested we talk about it later, first enjoy the afternoon.

"No unmarried couple is going to sleep behind a closed door on my dime."

I worried Kayla would say the obvious thing: We could mess around any night—at her apartment, which he paid for, or at mine. We could and we had—in the bedroom he paid for, the living room he paid for, and the bathroom he paid for.

The Baroness

We had all the privacy and opportunity we needed back home. Kayla said none of this, but she couldn't keep altogether quiet.

"We're on a family vacation, Dad. Nothing could be less sexy."

That adjective seemed to fill the room like steam. Saying less *romantic* would have been smart. The teenage girls drifted in from their room and circled over near Kayla's mother, who was opening and closing cupboards and drawers in the kitchenette and pretending not to hear. I walked to the window and looked out.

"We should get outside," I said. "It's amazing up here."

"We're grownups, Dad," Kayla said. "He shouldn't have to sleep on the couch."

I glanced at the sectional. The gray upholstery looked like it had been cleaned too often—it's texture raised and stiffened by the steam cleaner, or whatever they used to suck out the stains of ketchup, root beer, chocolate frosting, and smears of less innocence. I glanced into the cold stare of Kayla's father, then turned toward her.

"Here's how I see it, Kay." Her dad shifted forward, his body now alive with, I thought, hostility and suspicion. "People who want to be treated as grownups should behave like grownups."

Kayla gave me a here-we-go look.

"Grownups get married if they want to be a family of their own, if they want to have that status"—he made a broad circular gesture with his hands—"within the larger family."

The teenagers stared at me, waiting for a reply I was never going to make.

"But perhaps," Kayla's father continued, "perhaps it's just a matter of intentions. If you two plan on getting married, we could look at things differently. But if the relationship is nothing serious, we'll treat it that way."

"Forget it!" Kayla clapped her hands. "Let's go outside."

"So, tell us." Her dad looked at me. "Do you expect to marry Kayla, or are you just letting her keep you company?"

His question filled the room, but not like the steam Kayla had created. It felt like a cauldron of shit stew. I hoped he didn't expect me to reply, that he'd just been making a point. But he raised his eyebrows dramatically—like a curious mime you'd want to punch in the mouth. He'd cornered me, and he loved it.

"Well," I said, "I don't think this is the right occasion for a proposal."

"Oh, no," he said. "I'm only asking about your intentions."

"I said forget it," Kayla said. "I'll take the couch. A guest should get a bed."

"Nonsense." He dismissed Kayla with a wave of his hand. "Can't you even tell us what you intend?"

No one said anything. Kayla's dad stared at me. Each tick of silence only made me feel more screwed.

"I don't know what I intend," I said. "I don't think Kayla knows either."

Her father and I simultaneously turned toward Kayla, who bit her lip, shook her head, twisted her face toward the ceiling, and sniffed. She hadn't said a word, but everyone knew I had been wrong.

At first I tried to understand the pattern in a roll of five flavors. A cherry on top? Was there an orange below it? Did that mean a lemon or a lime followed? Seemed like there was a set pattern, like there had to be. What kind of factory would allow for randomness? None. Impossible. You never got three limes in row or anything surprising like that. There had to be a pattern, but I couldn't figure it out. I quit trying. I accepted it.

The four Heinekens I'd had that first night at the cabin seemed a safe bet to help me get to sleep quickly. But once the lights went out and I laid my head down, the empty minutes flowed into one another. Alone in the dark, I tried not to think about all the sweat and sunscreen and sand ground into the fabric. I tried not to think how utterly used everything felt. I positioned a blanket beneath my pillow—a resort blanket, I realized, which only made me consider the frequency of its trips to the laundry. Weekly? Monthly? Seasonally? I tossed it aside.

The teenage girls and Kayla's mother had gone to their rooms a couple hours earlier, all weary after a long day of travel and, finally, the lake and the sunshine. Kayla, her dad, and I sat around the table and drank his beer. He told stories about bringing Kayla north when she was just a kid—how she had baited her own hook when she was five, how she could swim like a fish even sooner than that, how she howled like a crazed raccoon when a leech attached itself between two of her toes. I smiled and looked admiringly at Kayla, which I supposed was my role in that situation.

When he asked if I wanted to come along fishing first thing tomorrow, I said, "Thanks, but I've never really been into fishing."

He looked at me like I was a heretic or a lunatic or someone else he didn't quite want around.

"He's a city kid, Dad," Kayla said.

He frowned and mumbled, "Different strokes."

Kayla and I were, I assumed, both hoping the same thing—that her dad would finally go to bed so we could steal some time together, just a few minutes to sit next to each other, to lean against each other and laugh about her mom and her dad and the stupid things they'd said.

"About time we call it a night," he said. "We'll be up early."

While her dad was in the bathroom, Kayla kissed me goodnight, only it wasn't one of her ordinary wet, slurping kisses. This one was neat and quick, and maybe that was sweet or maybe it was cold. I really didn't know.

Some light from the moon and stars came through the window, but everything inside looked indistinct—dark shapes beside other dark shapes. At least half an hour passed while I lay alone and listened to the world outside. A soft breeze sighed, and lake water rocked gently against the fishing boat, which groaned against the dock poles. I understood those sounds, but there was so much I didn't know. Bugs and birds moved around out there and made their noises, and I wondered who was saying what, wondered if I'd ever get to sleep, wondered what I was doing there.

Before I recognized the sound of her soft footsteps, Kayla nudged my shoulder, and I sat up. She wore a white T-shirt that draped down onto her thighs, and when she leaned to kiss me, I could see it was her father's gift to me the last Christmas. In diagonal script, it posed this question: "What if the hokey-pokey really is what it's all about?" She kissed me in her ordinary way—her tongue hard into my mouth and heavy against my teeth, lips, face, neck, earlobes. We moved quickly through our routine, and when she'd finished slobbering, she pulled me up, pulled me all the way back as she fell into the corner of the sectional. She hardly had to direct me. I slipped down, her hands on my shoulders, and knelt on the floor, the grit of it dimpling my skin. Her skin smelled like sand and lake water—an odor that was somehow fresh and fishy all at once.

I thought of pineapples and limes and all the sweet citrus packed tightly and cleanly into rolls. I rested my forehead on her hipbone and caught my breath. She put a hand in my hair. She kept so quiet, but her breaths shortened and muscles constricted.

I felt her body go rigid before I heard the footsteps. A switch clicked, and a wash of whiteness lit the room, the back of the sofa casting a shadow across Kayla's forehead. Stone still and silent, she stared down at me. Her eyes were those of a panicked kid.

"Kayla," said a soft voice from near the bathroom door. "Are you all right?"

The floor creaked, and footsteps came quickly. I had only enough time to pull Kayla's T-shirt over her lap. Her mother stopped behind the sectional, looked down, then jerked her face away. I sat up, elbows on Kayla's thighs. I wanted to talk us out of this spot, but no cover story would've made even a passable excuse. A guy got down on his knees for only a couple reasons, and we all knew this was no circumstance for the honorable one.

"It's okay," Kayla said. "Everything's okay."

Her mother replied, "You'd better get back to your room, honey."

Kayla and I had been together more than a year when I met the Baroness. She was a tall, solid woman, with big bones and broad shoulders and a swirl of blond hair curling back from the expanse of her forehead. She looked like a woman out of the past. She looked too good for me. She was a Republican.

My roommate had finally hooked me up with a new job—a temporary thing with the legislative Democrats. My job was to sit in committee hearings all day and write up summaries of debate on all bills, adding suggested talking points for our side and listing stupid things said by the opposition. Kayla's dad said it was foolish to leave one temp job for another, but he didn't know what he was talking about. There were two ways in at the Capitol—family connections or dues paid as session staff. I never had any family connections.

The Baroness introduced herself before a meeting of the Education Committee. We'd seen each other there every other day for two weeks, and at the Transportation Finance Subcommittee on the off days.

"We might as well be friendly," she said.

I didn't know what to say. I wondered if the Democrats on the committee might get suspicious if they saw me chatting up the other side. They didn't know me from Fritz Mondale.

"Good to meet you," I said. "Nice of you to say hi."

I sat down in the front row of the gallery, and the Baroness settled in one seat away. She smiled, pulled a stack of bills and summaries from her briefcase, and put on a pair of crooked glasses with round lenses and tortoise shell frames. She noticed me watching her and glanced my way.

"I'm always losing my glasses," she said. "These are old ones."

I wanted to say something witty. But that sort of thing was never a strength of mine.

"They're nice," I said. "They suit you."

The Baroness looked confused, as if she couldn't tell whether I was being sarcastic. I said, "Seriously," and she smiled.

Before he connected me with a job, Nate had joined the ranks of the few, the proud, the permanent. He even scored a tiny office with a door and a window overlooking a parking garage. I went to see him after I first met the Baroness at the committee meeting.

"What's the deal with that Republican researcher?" I asked.

"Which one?" He was at his desk, which was piled with newspapers from every corner of northern Minnesota. That was his turf, and those thin weeklies were everything to him. He wrote letters to the editor and op-ed pieces under the names of legislators from the Northland, and he sent them off to hometown papers. If his stuff got published—and it almost always did—he'd earned his pay. I coveted his job.

"Liz something. Big, solid chick. Blond hair. Forehead like Thomas Jefferson's."

"Elizabeth Enger," he said. "The Baroness."

I didn't have to ask about the nickname. It was perfect. Back then we knew the old movies. They still showed them on TV. This Liz was a serious figure, a high-class person. She was the Baroness.

I explained that I found her impressive, and my buddy agreed. She was no ordinary woman. She was put together like an old-time starlet, made of curves—serious curves. She might have been thirty or thirty-five. She might have been even older, but she looked fresh, alive, and real. She looked like a woman, not some expired college student with two new outfits and no idea how to behave, not like us. Her clothes were part of it. She wore a high-end woman's suit—skirt just above the knees, jacket fitted perfectly, blouse bright and smooth. Her shoes suffered no scuffs, her stockings no runs.

"She showed up last year. Got a permanent gig right away," Nate said. "Funny how that happens."

"She seems nice."

"Republicans have to act nice." He gave me a knowing glance. "Democrats have to act tough."

Sometimes Kayla and I would meet on Cathedral Hill when I finished work. We would have beers and cheeseburgers, and we would talk for hours. Sometimes we talked about her old boyfriend, her father's excesses and mother's compliance, her fatigue from working so much and going to school at the same time. Sometimes I drank a lot.

One night at Costello's Bar, we ate dinner and, for some reason, drank a bunch of daiquiris. Around midnight, we decided we'd have to walk home. On the sidewalk out front, I glanced up at the green dome of the Cathedral, looked down at Kayla's face, and followed a boozy impulse.

"Imagine if we had our wedding there." I nodded toward the massive church, lit brightly in a white glow. "Wouldn't that be amazing?"

Kayla walked on silently, her eyebrows bunched. Months had passed since the trip to the cabin, and she still looked injured whenever it came up, or when anyone mentioned anything having to do with marriage.

"You don't like that idea?" I knew I'd put myself out on a ledge, and I didn't care. I just wanted her to feel better, which seemed like a kind impulse even if I didn't fully believe what I was saying. "I'd be fine with whatever you want."

She kept silent as we walked. Half a block later, I decided I should be hurt about it.

"I'm serious here," I said. "And you've got nothing to say?"

Kayla stopped walking and pulled my hand so I'd stop and face her. As we stared at each other, I knew I'd made a mistake. She smiled. She beamed. Her eyebrows arched over wide, glistening eyes.

"I'm just surprised," she said.

One day I came in late and had to take the seat next to the Baroness. There was no space for our normal one-chair buffer. When she said hello, I tried but failed to repress a wince. She drank too much coffee, every day arriving with a large paper cup from the cafeteria, which she sipped through a plastic lid. Her breath stank like spent grounds in a day-old filter. This was her one flaw.

"Oh, God," she whispered, covering her mouth. "I'm sorry."

I smiled, pulled the Life Savers from my pocket, and peeled back the waxy paper. A lime one rested on top. I held the roll toward the Baroness.

"Oh, thank you." She popped it loose with her fingernail. "I love lime."

"They should make whole packs of lime," I whispered.

"They should." She set the candy on her tongue, then worked it around her mouth.

The next one was a pineapple. I put it in my mouth, stuffed the roll back into my pocket, and tried not to think about Kayla.

The Baroness

Kayla never knew the Baroness' real name—nor what she looked like or how much time I spent with her during my workdays. The Baroness never knew she had a nickname, never knew that most Democrats at the Capitol knew her no other way. The Baroness knew I had a girlfriend, but she might have made assumptions about the relationship based on my rare and sometimes wearied mentions of it. She never asked about Kayla, and I took that to mean something.

There must have been intention in the design. Those committee hearing rooms in the State Office Building were all the same—maroon carpeting, beige walls, beige upholstery in the galleries, dark woodwork, a massive table of the same dark wood at the focal point, black leather chairs around it. Those rooms were cruel. They gave you nothing to look at, nothing to daydream on. But there was the Baroness.

April nights went long, as committees piled up their spending bills and fought out the details. We could be the bullies, my side, because we had the votes. But it wouldn't be easy. Time had run short. Little work had gotten done. There was a Republican in the governor's office, and we all thought he was a prick.

The Baroness and I would stay as long as the reps did, late into the night. The meetings seemed endless. We sat side by side even if the gallery emptied after normal hours. We covered for each other's bathroom breaks, and we shared gum and mints and Life Savers. Some nights our small wagers kept us entertained. We'd bet a drink on which rep would be the first to nod off. The process of assembling multi-billion-dollar spending bills wasn't as exciting as it once sounded.

"I've got a gin and tonic that says Ness goes first," I said.

"Make it two," she said. "And I'll take Bertram."

Jerry Ness was a retired school principal from Thief River Falls, about as far from St. Paul as a person could get. He drove home most weekends and was known to be in a constant state of exhaustion, which didn't prevent him from embarking on long and confused oratories about obscure provisions of property tax law. And this effort seemed only to exhaust him more.

Tony Bertram from Duluth couldn't have bothered with home. He enjoyed long evenings in the lounge at the Kelly Hotel, his in-session place of residence. He'd grown notorious for collecting every possible dollar of per diem, which likely bankrolled his bar nights with groups of twenty-year-old pages and college interns.

We eyed the competitors carefully. The Baroness made notes in the margins of her pad, then reached it over my thigh so I could read and reply, making my notes there on her paper.

"Did you bring Life Savers?" she wrote.

"I'm not sharing," I jotted. "You take all my limes."

"Selfish, selfish!"

I pulled the nub of a roll from my pocket—three left and no backup supply. I handed her the pack, a coil of silver wrapping and wax lining sealing the top. She unwound the thing, and tore off the long tail. There rested a lovely little ring of light yellow, which the Baroness set on her tongue and savored, her cheek sucking in. She'd taken the pineapple. My mouth watered; my mind wandered.

She tapped her pad against my knee. She'd written, "Ness is going, going..."

At the far end of the table, the old guy sat back in his deep chair, chin on chest, head lolling sideways and jerking upright. I checked on her man and, my lips to her ear, whispered, "So is your guy."

The party boy's spot was two seats from the committee chair. No one could miss him. He had an elbow on the table and his forehead propped on his fist. He'd positioned himself as though intently reading a document, but his glasses had slipped halfway down his nose and his mouth drooped open. The competition turned into a slow ping-pong as the

The Baroness

Baroness and I watched for the first undeniable evidence of full slumber.

When Bertram's glasses finally fell and clacked onto the tabletop, the Baroness elbowed me hard. I let out a snort, which I tried to cover with a false cough. The party boy looked right at us. The Baroness kept her head down, but I felt her shoulder shake against mine. We sat red-faced and breathless, both staring at our notepads and trying to look busy.

A couple weeks before session adjourned, Kayla surprised me at work—showing up right at the end of the day and saying we were going on a date. She wanted to go to Cathedral Hill for beers and burgers at a place called Chang's. Lots of Capitol people did happy hour there. I worried we'd bump into the Baroness, but I went along. At the bar, I was uncomfortable and didn't have much to say. Halfway through the meal, I found myself tapping a half roll of Live Savers on the table and staring at a TV over Kayla's head.

"You sure go through a lot of those things," she said.

Distracted, I replied, "The Baroness eats half of them."

When I looked down at Kayla, I could see I'd made a mistake. Her eyebrows made a hard line over her narrowed eyes. I tried to talk us back and found myself explaining how the Baroness had coffee-breath issues, how I couldn't bear it some mornings, and how she always wanted the limes.

"Every day she shows up with a huge coffee in hand," I said. "It's gross."

"Do you sit by her every day?" Kayla asked.

"Sometimes we save each other seats," I replied. "It gets crowded, and we sort of try to help each other out."

"You only sit by her when it's crowded?" Kayla knew that sometimes the gallery for the Education Committee would be packed with angry parents or angry teachers or angry administrators, but other days there'd be only a few lobbyists and the caucus staff—the Baroness and me. I'd told her a lot about my new job.

"Well, you know, we're friends. We're friendly, I mean." I thought I'd leave it at that. Craning my neck, I sat up in my chair. "Where's that waitress? I need another drink. You want another Heineken?"

"Is that normal?"

"Huh?" I spotted the waitress but acted as though I hadn't. "Maybe I should just go up to the bar."

"Is it normal for Democrats and Republicans to be so friendly? Isn't that weird?"

Kayla's hands rested in her lap. She hadn't taken a bite or a sip since I mentioned the Baroness. She leaned forward, her chest level against the edge of the table. When she annoyed me, I couldn't help thinking how she looked like a wire doll—barely there, a thing that might break in half, only a girl, not a woman.

"It's like any office," I said. "You're stuck there together so you might as well get along."

"You talk about her a lot. Do you realize that?"

"Come on, Kayla." I smiled at her and rolled my eyes. "I see her every day. We're in the same hearings all time, and those hearings *are* my job. Should I not mention them?"

"You don't talk about committees or bills or that stuff." Kayla looked down at her half-eaten meal. "You talk about her."

The state constitution mandated that the Legislature adjourn no later than the Monday following the third Saturday in May. Late into the final night we waited for the education-funding bill to come back to the floor. The Baroness and I sat in the alcove at the back of the House chamber and waited with other staffers and unshaven newspaper reporters. A few minutes before

The Baroness

midnight, the speaker ordered that black cloth be draped over the clock. They would go until dawn if they had to.

"Come on," the Baroness said. "Let's get some air."

We sat on the top step in front of the Capitol. In the cool night, we settled in close together, hips touching. It felt entirely natural. We leaned lightly against each other, looking down at the long descent of white marble and the darkness of the lawn on the mall. Far below us was the city, rising across the freeway, which gave the night a backing hum from light traffic. The Capitol mall smelled of spring wetness and new grass. A June bug whirled above us and bounced against one of the old lanterns that lit the steps. There was nobody else around. I wanted to kiss her.

"I wonder when I'll get laid off," I said.

"Don't think about it," the Baroness said. "It's a perfect night. Just enjoy it. You'll want to remember this."

"What if we miss the bill?"

"They don't need us." She patted my knee. "Enjoy the night."

I couldn't. Right then I felt thirteen again, trying to figure how to make a move. Grab her hand? Put an arm around her and pull her closer? Put a hand on her thigh? A kiss would be too abrupt, and too risky. I was never any good at this, never any good at all. I decided I needed someone like Kayla, someone who took off her clothes and stood hands on hips, waiting for me to catch up. I never kissed a girl at thirteen. Not at fourteen, either.

The June bug tumbled downward, fluttered against my hair, and fell onto my lap. I leapt up and brushed it off. It landed on its back, skittering around in circles three steps down. I wanted to smash it with my heel. Laughing, the Baroness stood and backed away. I thought I knew what a man would do. I hurried down and scooped the bug into my hand, then tossed it into the air and watched it wobble toward the lantern again. Looking up at the Baroness, with the white glow of the building behind her, a smile on her face, I finally perceived the perfection of the night and knew I would want to remember the moment, to make it a snapshot I always carried around.

She reached a hand to me, and when I climbed toward her, she waited in place. I stopped one step below her, and she leaned down. The Baroness kissed gently, pleasantly. She parted her lips slightly, moved them softly against mine for small moments, then pulled me near. I kissed her neck.

She tightened her arms around me for a moment and said, "We should go."

I looked at her, and she nodded toward the Capitol doors.

As we hurried back through the building, I thought of dark and hidden corners we might use, but she kept an arm's length away and half a step ahead.

I said, "Liz, wait."

She glanced at me and smiled warmly, but continued walking with a business posture—moving quickly up the back stairs, through the clerk's office, and into the timeless chamber.

Anything at all could be charged with lust. If I put a pineapple Life Saver into my mouth, I thought of Kayla and the things we did together, things I'd never done with anyone else. Before her, Life Savers meant the pack of Pep-O-Mint fished from my grandmother's purse. Before her, Life Savers meant the Butter Rum roll left for months in a Christmastime book, left until my need for something sweet grew desperate. Anything at all could be stripped of innocence, and that was fine with me.

The layoffs came a week after adjournment, and we went to Chang's to drink our farewells. All of us session staffers were there, regardless of party, and some of the full-timers from both caucuses came to say goodbye. My buddy Nate stopped by and

The Baroness

bought a round for the two of us. The Baroness waved at me when she came in and sat at a table with some Republicans. She wore a light gray suit—the skirt and jacket and blouse just right, as always. You could tell the Republicans from the Democrats by the clothes.

"Stay cool," Nate said, sitting beside me at the bar. "Even if she liked you she wouldn't hang around you here."

"Even if," I said.

"What? You think she wants you?" He shook his head and smiled. "Dream on."

I hadn't told him about the favors we did each other, the games we played and laughs we had, or the night on the Capitol steps.

"I doubt it," I said. "But I wouldn't mind."

Happy hour ended and, one by one, people hugged and shook hands. Nate offered me a ride, but I said I'd take the bus. One more drink, then I'd catch a bus, no problem. I found a payphone outside the bathroom and left a message on Kayla's machine, promising to call again later and that's all. I didn't say where I was or why I was there. I wanted the night to myself.

When I got back to my spot, the Baroness took over the barstool beside me.

"You owe me a lot of drinks," she said. "I lost count, but I know it's a lot."

"You got it," I said. "Two gin and tonics, coming right up."

"And what'll you have?" she said.

We laughed together, and I wanted to say something crazy—wanted to tell her she was magnificent, that I'd gone nuts for her, that I would sit forever in a purgatory of legislative hearings if I could do it alongside her. But I wasn't drunk enough to say those things, not yet drunk enough. I only laughed and raised my hand to the bartender.

The Baroness had driven us back to my apartment because she agreed with my suggestion: "We deserve a nightcap." She should not have driven, but she did. And, as I mixed more gin and tonics in my kitchen, I told her she had done well. She waited in the living room and talked loudly and regretfully about what we'd just done, the danger of it. The machine on the countertop showed four messages waiting. As I stared at the flashing light, I urged the Baroness to give herself a break—she'd driven just fine and everything was great.

I came around the corner and saw her there, sitting on the edge of the couch in her blouse and skirt. She'd taken off her jacket and laid it neatly on the back of a chair. The light fabric of her blouse strained against her shape, and the shadow of her bra, one of those heavy-duty models, showed though. She smiled as I walked over and handed her the drink.

"This is the last thing we need," she said, but took a long sip.

"I made them a little weak," I said, sitting down close to her.

"How am I going to get home?"

"I can call a cab," I said. "Or you can stay here."

She stared at me, her eyes red-rimmed, and smirked. I couldn't tell if she looked weary or content. I leaned and kissed her, trying to remember the way things had gone on the Capitol steps, not wanting to get it wrong. First we kissed like roller-rink kids—pecking and whispering and leaning our heads together. As we matured, I let her lead the way. She kissed with parted lips. Her tongue moved shyly, and it felt calm and warm. I thought this must be the right way.

In my room, we lay down on top of the covers and kept on kissing, kissing, kissing. She untucked my shirt and moved her warm hands across my back, and I did the same to her. We kissed slowly and rested and let our eyes close. I never knew who fell asleep first.

The Baroness

I dreamed of Jenny Herbert, the junior high girl who took me into a dark closet with her, who raised my fingers to her lips so I would know where to look when she chomped a mouthful of Wint-O-Green Life Savers. "Watch for the sparks," she said, and as the candy cracked and crunched between her teeth, I said, "I see 'em. I see sparks." But it was a lie—a lie told in hopes she wouldn't figure out that I couldn't even do that right, couldn't even see candy make sparks, which everyone knew only Wint-O-Green Life Savers could do.

When the pressure grew painful enough to wake me, even from a deep and boozy sleep, I eased off the bed so I wouldn't wake Liz. The sight of her—the beautiful Baroness—sleeping there gave me a thrill, a jolt of delight that roused my mind. In the bathroom, I pissed a long night's worth of piss, and I said a little prayer that she wouldn't hear me blasting away and be disgusted.

As I finished up, a tapping sound echoed from the other room—three soft but distinct taps. I left the toilet unflushed and leaned toward the door. My ears fizzed after the hours in a noisy bar. I wondered if I'd heard anything at all, but three more raps came down the hall. No mistaking where they came from now.

I switched off the light and tiptoed into the dark hallway. I focused on my breathing and my footsteps, trying to keep silent. Darkness filled the apartment except for the line of white light along the bottom of the door leading out—a door I knew I'd locked. I heard three more knocks, louder this time, then the shuffling sounds of Liz stirring on the bed. The knocking kept up—faster and louder, knuckles rapping against wood, the rattling of the door against its hinges.

I moved to the doorway of my bedroom, where the Baroness got up and smoothed her skirt. She switched on the lamp, glanced at me, and tugged the bottom of her blouse to straighten it. After pushing her hair behind her ears, she patted her bangs back off of her forehead.

"What's going on?" She did not whisper. "Why don't you get the door?"

"Shhh," I said. "If we just keep—"

"Who's in there?" Kayla's voice muffled in. She knocked again and said, "I can hear you."

"Shhh," I said again, as I stepped into the bedroom. "It'll be okay."

"No, you can't do this." Liz's face looked gray and tired—her eye shadow dimmed, mascara slightly smeared, and lipstick gone except faint lines at the corners of her mouth. "She knows you're here."

"Maybe," I said. "But she doesn't know you're here."

Kayla banged against the door again and called my name.

Liz sighed and said, "Am I supposed to hide under the bed?"

I glanced at the narrow space beneath the bed frame and looked back at Liz, whose pinched expression told me I'd made another mistake.

"Fine," I said. "Wait here."

A series of solid thuds came from the door, outside of which Kayla must have given up knocking and started kicking. The noise stopped when I switched on a living room light. I unlocked the front door and cracked it.

"What's going on?" Kayla looked half-nuts. She wore one of my windbreakers and some sweat pants, and coils of her hair fell over her eyes. "Where have you been?"

"We got laid off today." I spoke through a narrow gap. "We all went and got drunk."

"Let me in," Kayla said.

"Shhh." I held the door against Kayla's weight. "You're waking the whole building."

"Don't shush me!" she half-grunted as she tried to push her way in.

The Baroness

I ignored the sound of Liz's footsteps as she came out of the bedroom and into the living room. She plucked her jacket from the chair and said, "Let her in."

Kayla quit pushing and stepped back as I let the door swing open. The three of us kept still. I looked at Kayla, then back at Liz. Kayla looked at me, then at the woman in my living room. Liz looked at us—my girlfriend and me—and shook her head.

"I knew it," Kayla said softly. "That's the Baroness, isn't it?"

"What?" Liz said.

"Nothing," I said. "Come on, Kay, let's talk about—"

"What did she call me?" Liz asked.

I couldn't think of a thing to say.

"That's her, isn't it?" Kayla said. "I knew it. I *knew* it."

I'd never been so utterly screwed in my life, never been served such a shit sandwich as this, and I could think of no excuse or apology worth the breath. I stood there. I said nothing. When Liz pulled on her jacket and strode between Kayla and me, I didn't try to stop her. I looked at Kayla. Her reddened, tense-jawed face showed a different beauty than I'd seen before. I looked at that face and saw hostility and heartbreak—nothing masking them, all wide open and honest. I looked at that face and felt happy Kayla still hadn't walked away. Not yet, not yet.

Close Relations

Lorraine sat on a stout retaining wall outside the Health Department and watched for her daughter to come by in the station wagon. The sidewalk remained clean and slick from an early morning rain that had washed away the last traces of snow, except for some blackened chunks of ice packed hard in the shadows. Lorraine didn't mind that the concrete beneath her rear end was damp. She needed to get off her feet.

As she rested, Lorraine unfolded the document in her hand and read it for a second time. The page was a photocopy; its ink had not really been left by the doctor's pen. Still, she ran a fingertip over the letters—all coils and barbs, nearly impossible to decipher—and thought how she despised the man who had written the words. He had dashed off his notes without regard for the baby or for her family, with no concern for their feelings. He hadn't even taken time to make sure another person would be able to read his script.

The death certificate described the condition of a malformed infant, known in the records only as Baby Girl Anderson. As far as Lorraine could tell, the doctor who delivered her sister had held in his hands something not fully developed. No skin or muscle had formed over the girl's midsection, leaving internal organs visible in their cavity. Similar problems afflicted her face. Lorraine couldn't make out all the words, but she could read "eyes absent of lids" clearly enough.

The concluding line of the doctor's notes was unmistakable. He had taken his time there, shaping each letter crisply and forming two words that were half again as large as the scribbles preceding them. The doctor's final declaration had been this: "A monstrosity." Lorraine read the words again out loud and felt tightness in her throat.

She folded the paper into quarters, stood up, and slipped it into her raincoat pocket just as Vicki turned the corner and jerked to a stop at the curb. Little Austin's head swayed against his safety seat, and he craned his neck to get a look out the window. Rock music thumped through the glass.

"Could you please turn that down?" Lorraine half-shouted as she swung open the door and bent into the passenger seat. "You're going to burst that child's eardrums."

"He loves this tune," Vicki said, her head bobbing in time to the song, which sounded to Lorraine like the type of thing played by musicians who would smash their instruments when they were finally through.

Lorraine reached over and twisted the volume knob. The station wagon belonged to her. It was an expensive vehicle made in Sweden, easily the most extravagant thing Lorraine had ever owned, and she hadn't bought it so she could suffer. She set the music to a level that would allow them to talk in normal voices.

"No!" Austin howled from the backseat. "Make it loud. Make it loud."

Vicki hit the gas before her mother had time to buckle up and jerked the wagon back into traffic heading into the center of St. Paul.

"You should use your signal," Lorraine said.

"Give me a break, Mom," Vicki said.
"Make it loud," Austin said. "Make it loud."
"Let's all quiet down," Lorraine said, "so you can hear the music."
Her daughter added, "Grandma doesn't like it loud."
"Grandma's stupid," Austin said. "Stupid shithead."
Lorraine sighed and pretended to ignore her grandson. She whispered to Vicki, "Where does he get that language?"
"Where do you think?" Vicki answered.
Lorraine nodded, understanding she was meant to believe the boy had acquired his vocabulary from Wayne, his father and Vicki's longtime on-again, off-again boyfriend.
Vicki added, "You know the mouth on that dumb ass."
"Indeed," Lorraine said.

Nearly two years earlier, Lorraine and her husband, Jim, had gone to dinner at Mancini's Char House to mark her sixtieth birthday. She suggested the place because her parents had liked to go there for special occasions, and while she wasn't sure, Lorraine thought her father had celebrated his final birthday with a big Mancini's steak and all the garlic toast he could eat. Her father died at sixty, one long month after his lung-cancer diagnosis, and Lorraine couldn't help thinking about him as she neared that age herself.

"I don't remember coming here for his last birthday," Jim said as they sat in the dim dining room and waited for the waitress to come by with their wine. "I don't remember anything about his birthday at all."

"Of course you don't," Lorraine said. "We didn't know it was going to be the last one."

"But you remember it?"

"Not for certain," Lorraine said.

A busboy dropped a basket of garlic toast on the table, and Jim reached for a piece. There were two types, white and dark bread, all of it singed with black grill marks and soaked with melted garlic butter. Jim preferred the white, and Lorraine liked the dark. She'd always thought they were a good fit that way.

"It's so hard to recall anything for certain," Lorraine said. "I remember coming here for his birthday once when the kids were getting to be bigger. I remember it clearly because my mother suggested we get a sitter and I'd gotten hurt feelings over that."

"Why?" Jim spoke with his cheek full of food, and he reached for another piece of bread. He ate with the speed and appetite of a farmhand, which annoyed Lorraine. Jim had packed on fifty pounds since they were married, but tonight he looked his best. He wore his navy sports jacket, which pleased Lorraine because it brought out the blue in his eyes and reminded her of the young man she once knew, the man with a full head of blond hair, a trim waist, and one chin.

"Because they were good kids," Lorraine said, "And I wished Mom would want them around."

Jim furrowed his brow as he chewed.

"Silly," Lorraine said. "I know that now, but it was something that upset me at the time. My mother behaved like she wasn't much interested in the kids when they were little, when they might have wanted something from her—like a clean diaper or a bottle of milk or a peanut butter and jelly with the crusts cut off."

"Come on, now," Jim said. "Let's not go down that old road. Let's have a nice time."

The waitress came with the wine. Just in time, Lorraine thought as she took a long sip that was not at all ladylike. Her husband smiled.

"Easy there," he said.

Lorraine laughed. "I know," she said. "You're right. I'll drop it. It's just that they've been on my mind, Mom and Dad. They've been on my mind a lot lately."

"I can tell."

"It's just that people go around like every day is merely another day, like everything will always be the same, or maybe it'll only get easier with time," Lorraine said. "Then you wake up one day and half the people in your life are gone, and you realize you hardly knew each other."

This sort of thing happened with Vicki, Lorraine knew. You ask her to help you out with some errands. You suggest the two of you could make a day of it—head to the Health Department in the morning, have some lunch downtown, and search out your sister's grave in the afternoon. She says fine, she'll get a sitter, and it'll be nice. Then the day comes, and Vicki shows up half an hour late with Austin at her side and a long story about how she needs you to babysit while she goes to a chiropractic appointment she had completely forgotten about. And as long as she is going all the way to Minneapolis for the appointment, she ought to grab a bite with her friend who works over there and whom she hasn't seen in ages. She figures you wouldn't mind watching Austin.

Lorraine had hardly bothered getting upset about it. All she asked was that Vicki drive her downtown to the Health Department, circle the block while she ran in for the certificate, and bring her back home.

Once they'd returned, Vicki hurried off to her appointment, and Lorraine took Austin inside. She set him up with a grilled cheese sandwich and milk stirred with chocolate syrup, clicked on the kitchen television for him, and sat at the dining room table to make a call. The death certificate listed Birchwood Cemetery—a name she hadn't recognized. The listing in the phone book gave a Woodbury address, far east of the city and distant from anywhere her family had ever lived and any of the cemeteries that held her parents, grandparents, and other relatives.

A man with a friendly voice answered at the cemetery, and Lorraine found herself telling him the whole story. She had been working on her genealogy for a year now, and she'd finally decided to find out what had happened to her younger sister, a matter her parents had never said much about and, in fact, had seemed to want to forget. She had thought first to find her sister's grave, but that had proven difficult. The family name was Anderson, and it turns out the cemeteries aren't short on Baby Girl Andersons, even when you can narrow the time of death down to a year and a season—fall of 1955. A man at another cemetery had suggested she get a copy of the death certificate.

"I understand," said the man at Birchwood. "So you've got the document now?"

"Yes, she's in your cemetery," Lorraine said.

The man asked for the date of death and the parents' names, and put Lorraine on hold. She kept the phone to her ear and peeked into the kitchen, where Austin drank from his chocolate milk, most of which dribbled down his chin and onto his yellow turtleneck. He looked like quite the little Swede in that color, with his skin a pale pink and hair a nearly pure white—just like Vicki's had been as a child—and his baby blue eyes. His face often wore a forlorn expression—something in the arc of his eyebrows—that made her want to hug him and pat his head and tell him he was a good boy. Then he would open his mouth and speak, and she would often want to throw up her hands in defeat to the profane world that had infused itself into her grandchild.

When he came back on the line, the cemetery man's voice startled Lorraine. Her gasp made him chuckle, and then he told Lorraine the section, row, and plot number for her sister's grave. She felt a mixture of embarrassment and satisfaction when she hung up, returned to the kitchen, and swept some crumbs from the tabletop into her hand.

"Let's finish up," she said. "We're going to the flower shop, and then we're going to visit my sister."

"My sister?" Austin spoke with one cheek bulging and food in his teeth, just like his grandfather.

"Not your sister, silly," Lorraine said. "Mine."

"What's her name?"

Lorraine ignored the question. "Anyway," she said, "you don't have a sister."

"Uh-huh," he said. "She's in Mommy's tummy."

One Saturday not long after her sixtieth birthday, Lorraine went to the store and bought a computer program that the salesman promised would help her gather and organize the facts of her genealogy. She would assemble all the information about her family first, going back to when her mother's people came from Ireland and her father's people came from Sweden. Then she would do the same for Jim's side, tracing them back to Sweden on father's side and Norway on his mother's side.

"Then I'll print off a copy for each of the kids," she told Jim. "Maybe I'll get some nice paper and put together a three-ring binder for each of them. They can add to it later if they want, or just put it away for their own kids to have when they're grown."

The two of them sat at the kitchen table, and Jim eyed the shrink-wrapped box holding the software. He wore his pajamas even though it was nearly noon, as he often did on weekends, and a half-finished crossword puzzle lay in front of him.

Sunshine filled the room, and Lorraine thought how she enjoyed the spring and how it made their home feel like a happier place. She still had on her coat, the same beige raincoat she'd been wearing in the spring and fall for years. She liked it because it held up and because it wasn't too wide in the shoulders, which was a problem for someone with a frame like hers. She thought she might be due for a new one, but she hadn't been able to find another like it. When she looked through the window at a chickadee on the birdfeeder in the backyard, Lorraine couldn't help but grin.

"Sixty-nine dollars seems like an awful lot, don't you think?" Jim asked.

"That's how much these things cost," Lorraine said.

"Sure." Jim tipped back in his chair, which creaked beneath him. The metal frame of the chair pressed against the wall in a spot where over the years it had chipped and rubbed away the yellow paint. "I'm just saying you could do this just as well on your own. I mean I don't see why a family tree is so complicated that you need a computer to draw it up for you."

"It's not just a list of names," Lorraine said. "It's family history. This will keep all the dates and names and places, plus all the stories of these people. It'll all be together. It'll be like a book. You'll see."

Jim sniffed and chewed his lower lip, and Lorraine knew he was preparing one of his monologues, one of his rambling speeches that would refute everything she had said and leave no room for her to argue when he was through.

"If you ask me," he began, "this entire genealogy craze is a futile exercise. If our ancestors have meant so little to us that we don't even know when they were born and died, why bother scratching around for all these facts just so you can type them into a computer? Why pour hours of time—"

"Nobody asked you, Jim." Lorraine plucked the software box from his hand and got up from the table. "All I wanted you to do was to put this onto the computer for me."

Computers, after all, were Jim's area of expertise. He'd been with his company since what he called the "vacuum-tube days," had endured several corporate makeovers and name changes, and had survived round after round of downsizing. By now, he managed his department and earned a good enough living to allow Lorraine to quit her job as lunch lady and playground monitor at the neighborhood elementary school and to buy herself a nice car, the kind she wished for when the kids were little.

"Now don't get hurt," he said. "I was only saying that those people are dead and gone now, and most of them haven't meant a thing in our lives."

"How'd you like it if your grandchildren or great grandchildren said that someday?" Lorraine asked.

"That's just it." Jim rocked forward in his chair, his eyes wide, and thumped the table with a loose fist. "That's what this is all about—people convincing themselves their lives will have meaning after they're dead. But that's baloney. You get this life, you make what you can of it, and you're gone."

The clouds returned after lunchtime, and by the time they arrived at the flower shop, drizzle streaked the windshield of the station wagon. Vicki hadn't left a slicker or rubber boots for her son, and Lorraine wasn't keen on letting him tromp around in his sneakers and jean jacket on a wet day. But she was determined to see her plans through. She was not going to let Vicki's haphazard way of living get in the way again.

Austin held his grandmother's hand in the parking lot and hopped most of the way from the car to the doorway. Lorraine explained that they needed to hustle, that he should keep his hands to himself inside the shop, and that maybe they would have time to stop for a treat on the way home if he used his best behavior.

"Can I pick the flowers?" Austin asked.

"What kind of flowers do you like?"

"Let me pick 'em," Austin said.

"Do you mean, '*Please*, let me pick them?'"

The boy did not respond. When they got inside, he looked around, headed for the coolers holding fresh-cut flowers, and pressed his nose against the glass. His shoulders slumped, and he let out a groan as he laid his weight against the glass case. Only then did it dawn on Lorraine that Austin had expected to walk into a flowerbed and pick a handful of stems from the soil. She laughed.

"Sorry, kiddo," she said. "Help me choose some pretty ones."

He shook his head, and when she tried to coax him into pointing out his favorites, he crossed his arms on his chest and turned his back. She asked the clerk for a dozen carnations—six yellow and six light blue—and one of those holders you stick into the grass at the cemetery. The clerk knew just the thing, and she trimmed the stems short so the flowers would stand up nice and straight.

Austin kept quiet on the twenty-minute ride to the cemetery. Lorraine could imagine only two reasons her father might have chosen to bury the child so far from home: Either the price was right, or he wanted the baby someplace distant and unfamiliar, where her family wouldn't have to be reminded of her. That was the way that man thought. He believed his stoicism was his finest virtue. He thought it made life better for his family. He really believed that.

Lorraine found the cemetery without trouble, but once inside the gates, she became confused. The narrow roads curved in all directions without any rhyme or reason, and the section markers—narrow white posts with green letters—were difficult to spot. Austin complained and strained against the straps of his car seat. The drizzle outside had grown to a light but steady rain.

"Out, out, out," he said. "Let me out, Grandma."

"Settle down, Honey."

"Grandma's stupid." He started bawling and grunting, yanking on the buckle between his legs. "Grandma's a stupid shithead!"

Lorraine sighed and mumbled, "No treat for you, mister."

After five minutes of wrong turns, she found section six—not far from the entrance. She parked the car half on the lawn, which was still brown and matted in early spring, and released Austin from his seat. His face was red from all his wiggling and whining. Lorraine handed him the bundle of flowers, and they walked together to a water faucet at end of the front row. She put the flower stand under the spout and cranked on the knob, but nothing came out.

"What's wrong?" Austin asked. He reached up and turned the knob back and forth.

"They haven't turned the water back on," she said. "They shut it off in wintertime, so the pipes don't freeze."

Austin cranked the faucet back and forth, gave up, and followed her to Row D, where she turned right and walked ahead with her eyes on the ground. She stopped at an unusually wide gap between two headstones, and toed the grass with her shoe until it hit something hard. Then she bent and brushed the dead grass away from the tiny piece of unpolished stone no larger than three inches square. The stone bore the marking "D17."

"This is the place," she said.

Austin kneeled down and pulled the rest of the grass away from the marker, yanked it up by the roots, leaving a fresh ring of damp brown soil surrounding the stone. Lorraine pressed the prongs of the flower holder into the soil and asked Austin to place the flowers inside. He did his job gently, then stood up—the knees of his trousers dark with water and dirt—and stepped back to admire what they'd done.

The computer keys clacked beneath Lorraine's fingertips as she entered the new data. Seen this way, the life of her younger sister was a simple enough thing. She had suffered serious physical defects; she could not survive on her own. Her lifespan passed someplace in St. Joseph's hospital, surely someplace away from the healthy boys and girls in the nursery, who were watched through the glass by smiling fathers and grandparents and siblings.

Lorraine worked at the computer in an otherwise empty bedroom where her older girl had once slept. An afghan—an ivory-colored one her mother knitted years ago—lay across her lap as she worked. She had gotten the hang of the genealogy software, which Jim installed on the computer despite his complaints about the cost. She still had a great deal of work to do on her ancestry, but this felt like an important step, filling in the blank in her own family, in the household where she'd been raised.

Jim tapped on the open door and spoke from the hallway, where he stood in a nylon jogging suit, the sort he'd taken to wearing every day after work and on weekends. "What'd you find out today?" he asked.

Lorraine didn't know how to answer that question. She hadn't yet thought of a full yet simple way of explaining what she'd come to know about her sister.

"I know where she's buried." Lorraine paused her typing. She glanced over her shoulder, and went back to looking at the screen. "She's out in Woodbury."

"Woodbury?" Jim shifted his weight and leaned in the doorframe. His jogging suit swished with every move. "What's she doing way out there?"

"Good question," Lorraine said. "You know my dad. I'm sure he had his reasons."

Jim snorted. "Sure," he said. "He must have known a guy who knew a guy who could get him the plot for a song."

Lorraine shrugged. It occurred to her that Jim knew he was saying something that, while quite possibly true, was better left unsaid. He had some compulsion to behave like the cold seer and speaker of the truth, and he couldn't or wouldn't recognize how the things he said could hurt people. Deep inside, she felt it was Jim's fault that their two older children had moved out of state—not so much that he had driven them away, more that he had never encouraged them to stay. Anyway, the older kids had gone off and found happiness far from home, and the only child who came around with regularity was the one who still depended on Jim and Lorraine—mostly Lorraine—for so much.

When Lorraine didn't respond, Jim said, "Well, then, I'll let you get back to work."

Lorraine listened to him swish off down the hallway. She read the information she'd typed in so far and thought about how she might summarize the contents of the death certificate, which lay unfolded on the desk next to the keyboard. She wanted to include enough detail so her children and grandchildren might someday understand what really happened to her baby sister, but she struggled to find words other than those of the doctor.

She read the doctor's notes again, and she thought how good it was that her mother hadn't known her child was described this way. Lorraine's mother—herself gone ten years now—had never really seen the baby at all, had not been forced to live with a mind full of images of that poor, small body. She had glimpsed a figure in a nurse's hands as the baby was rushed out of the delivery room. That's all.

Lorraine heard the story only once—soon after Vicki was born. Vicki's birth had been long and difficult, and when the doctor finally pulled her into the world, she was bruised all over, scraped by forceps, and blue from lack of oxygen. The family worried in the early days that she might have suffered some lasting damage, that she might never be right.

With Vicki off in the nursery and Lorraine resting in her hospital room, her mother sat down on the edge of the mattress and rested a hand on the blanket over Lorraine's leg. She rubbed back and forth along the shin until Lorraine felt the warmth of her mother's hand come through the material. Her mother said everything was going to be okay, that the doctors could do so much more these days.

"Things were different when your sister was born," she said. "There was nothing they could do for her."

Lorraine lifted her head off the pillow and leaned toward her mother, who was by then in her fifties, a frail woman who folded her pale green overcoat on her lap and left a white scarf in her gray hair, as she often did in the spring. Surprised to hear her mother speak of the lost baby, Lorraine hadn't known what to say.

"In those times, they just took the baby away," Lorraine's mother said. "They never let you see it, much less hold it in your arms."

Her mother looked at the floor as she spoke. She stared toward the quiet corridor outside the hospital room. She kept a hand on Lorraine's shin. Lorraine thought to put a hand on top of her mother's, but she didn't want to upset her.

"You could have a fine pregnancy, everything just as it should be, and never know anything was wrong," Lorraine's mother said. "Then your baby is born, you see a nurse with tears in her eyes, the doctor is telling her to go, and she has got a bundle in her arms when she goes. That's all."

"Mom," Lorraine said. "Why didn't you ever tell me?"

"People did not discuss these things," her mother said. "People did not go around saying anything that came to mind to anyone who would listen like they do now. You swallowed it. You had to."

At her desk, Lorraine drew a deep breath and shook her head, forcing her mind back to the task at hand. Lifting the death certificate nearer to her eyes, Lorraine rocked back in her chair and read the doctor's notes another time. Again she followed the curls and kinks of his letters, imagined his pen moving over the paper. Then she noticed something she'd missed before. There, at the bottom of the page, was the jumble of her own father's signature.

After leaning on her mother for babysitting during two monthly visits, Vicki finally confessed that she hadn't been at the chiropractor at all. She'd been at the obstetrician. She decided to tell Lorraine this news while the two of them sat at a table in the McDonald's

Playplace and watched Austin zip out of a plastic tube onto the padded floor. He scrambled to his feet and began climbing up through the two-story apparatus of tubes, ladders, and slides, rushing upward so he could zoom down again. The room was alive with the noise of children running, climbing, and hollering, along with parents chattering, cautioning, and hollering, too.

"I'm due in September," Vicki said. "The fourteenth."

Lorraine first wondered who might be the baby's father. She hoped he was Wayne, who had been ready and willing to marry Vicki since before their son was born, nearly three years ago now. Wayne and Vicki had broken up and reunited half a dozen times before that pregnancy and at least as many times since. Their troubles were mostly Vicki's doing. She said she wasn't interested in being anybody's wife, that she was whole and needed nobody else to make her feel complete. That Wayne shrugged off such talk had always surprised Lorraine.

"Goodness," she said, without looking at her daughter. "That's big news."

"You don't sound very excited," Vicki said.

Lorraine knew her daughter was right, and she wished it wasn't so. She studied Vicki, who slouched forward with her arms folded over her chest, and thought how lovely her girl had turned out, how Vicki had the same thin frame and gentle hands as her grandmother. Vicki's eyes, wet and blinking, did not meet Lorraine's. She sat up, pushed her pale hair behind her ears, and gave a forced smile.

"Anyway, Austin will be happy to have a playmate," she said.

"Sure he will," Lorraine said, deciding to proceed under the assumption Wayne was the father unless she heard otherwise. "It's wonderful, Vicki. It's just wonderful."

A rumbling sound rose from within the red tube that formed the longest and curviest of the slides, and the racket ended when Austin shot from the bottom and slammed to the floor, face first against the thin foam. Vicki sprang up, dashed to the boy, and crouched over him. Lorraine followed.

Austin rolled over and lay silent, staring dull-eyed toward his mother, who reached to touch his forehead and asked if he was okay. He drew a short breath and released a long screech. The screech sank into a steady, whining howl.

"You're okay, buddy," Vicki said. She glanced at Lorraine and said, "He's just embarrassed."

Lorraine and Vicki smiled at each other, which did not escape Austin's notice. He jerked away from them.

"You stupid, Mommy!" he yelled. "You a stupid shithead."

The other parents and children quieted, and Lorraine felt many eyes on her and her family. She shushed Austin and told him it was only an accident, that there was no reason to be angry.

He covered his face with his hands and curled his small body into a ball.

"Shut up, Grandma!" he said. "You a shithead, Grandma. You a stupid shithead, too."

Vicki snatched Austin from the floor and pulled him hard against her chest when he tried to wiggle away.

"We're out of here," she said.

"Good Lord, what next?" Lorraine said. She looked around the room and saw people pretending not to notice.

Vicki lugged Austin toward the door, with him sobbing now and straining to get free. To her mother, she said, "Just grab my keys and my jacket, and let's get the fuck out of here."

Lorraine hadn't expected the credit card statement to come so quickly, and she hadn't given it a thought when Jim sat down at the kitchen table to do the bills. She stood at the sink and washed their dinner plates and water glasses, and the two of them chatted while they worked. Lorraine twisted the dishrag down into a tall tumbler, looked out at the gray twilight beyond the glass of the window above the sink, and listened to Jim complain about the amount of each bill. He said each one was outrageous, ridiculous even. It was the same way each month.

"What's this?" he said. "What in hell? Five hundred ninety-five dollars?"

Jim's words didn't immediately register with Lorraine. She went on washing, enjoying her work the way she enjoyed most of the peaceful routines of keeping a house.

"Lorraine," Jim said. "I'm asking you a question."

"What is it?"

"I said, 'What in hell are you charging for five hundred ninety-five dollars at Flannery Stone and Monument?'"

Lorraine shut off the tap and stared at Jim while she dried her hands. She had been trying to think of a way to explain this to him for a couple weeks now, and she still didn't know quite what to say. She wanted him to grasp the necessity of this. She needed him to understand why it mattered. She knew he wasn't given to such thinking.

"I bought a grave marker for my sister," she said. "It's not much, just a flat stone with her name on it."

"Her name?" Jim peered at her over the top of his drugstore reading glasses. "I didn't think she had one."

"I felt strongly about doing this, but I didn't think you'd understand," Lorraine said.

"Well, you're right, I don't understand," Jim said. "I don't understand why nobody gave it a second thought for fifty years, and now you can't wait to spend five hundred ninety-five dollars for a stone on a grave nobody ever visited before."

"It seems like the least you can do for a person," she said, "to recognize there was a life there."

Jim shook his head. He tore the voucher from the credit-card statement, and while Lorraine watched, he scratched out a check for the full amount. His movements were big and grand. He signed his name in huge, sloppy script, stuffed the papers into the envelope, slid his tongue over the flap, and slapped it closed.

"There," he said. "It's done."

"I'm glad," Lorraine said.

"You realize that up in heaven your father is now rolling his eyes," Jim said.

Lorraine smiled. She would explain later about the cemetery's installation fee.

Her father's signature on the death certificate put Lorraine to thinking. She thought mostly of him and his silence. She wondered what other truths he had known in life and kept to himself. In idle moments—alone on the freeway or at night in her bed—she let her imagination go to work. She created for herself a possible history of her sister's life and her father's involvement in it.

For years, all she had known of that child's brief spell on Earth was what her mother told her. Lorraine had imagined the delivery room scene her mother described—the look on the doctor's face, the figure in the nurse's arms, the quick exit—and concluded that the rest of her sister's short life had gone like this: The nurse whisks the girl to a private room, where she swaddles her and sets her in a solitary crib, and as the nurse watches, the child labors for breath but soon gives up the work. This was the story Lorraine had told herself whenever the thought of her lost sister came to mind.

The death certificate demanded a rewrite of this account. Lorraine decided her father must have been summoned by the doctor and that her father would have gone into that room where the baby lived her three hours. Lorraine imagined her dad, a lean and slow-moving man with narrow shoulders, seated in a chair near the crib. She saw him dressed in one of his dark suits, his overcoat draped over the seatback.

The baby would have been wrapped, held together in places by mummy-like gauze, and she would have cried until her strength ran out. For three hours, her father and her sister were together, Lorraine believed. For three hours, her father watched his daughter die. He might have reached a hand into the crib—he had long hands—and touched with one finger the open palm of his girl.

"Now, now," he would have said, as he always said to unhappy children. "That's enough now."

Austin ate scrambled eggs off the floor beneath the kitchen table while Lorraine talked on the telephone. She had watched him bump his bowl from the tabletop, look around, and climb off his chair, and she assumed he meant to clean up his mess. This pleased her, until he began plucking up the larger puffs of yellow eggs from the linoleum and popping them onto his tongue. She mouthed *No! No!*, but Austin chewed away happily.

She didn't want to interrupt the cemetery man, who was calling to explain that the headstone had been installed and that he had billed all services to her credit card. She asked how the marker looked, and the man explained that he hadn't been over to see for himself but he was sure it was fine.

"I'll make the trip out," Lorraine said. "I'm pleased to know it's there."

She and her grandson were alone together again that morning. Vicki had gone off to another appointment, and Jim was at work. The bright May sunshine made the air coming in through open windows smell of warm and wet soil.

"Looks like we're off on another field trip," Lorraine said. "Are you almost through down there?"

Austin nodded and crawled out from under the table. Vicki had dressed him in beige shorts, which seemed a bit premature, and a light blue sweatshirt with a large hood, which he wore over his hair even indoors.

As Lorraine loaded Austin into the backseat of her station wagon, Vicki's Jeep rattled into the driveway and stopped. Lorraine shut the rear door and walked to Vicki's window, where she waited for her daughter to turn down her radio and roll down the glass. Instead Vicki nodded for her mom to step aside, bounced out of the door, and slung her purse over her shoulder.

"Where you headed?" Vicki asked.

She didn't behave like a pregnant woman, and she sure didn't look like one. To Lorraine's eye, she still looked like a skinny and clumsy teenager, dressed in tennis shoes and jogging suits, going around with her hair held in a ponytail by a rubber band.

"To the cemetery. Would you like to come along?"

Vicki smirked. "You sure know how to show a kid a good time."

On the freeway through the city and the eastern suburbs, Lorraine let her daughter choose the radio station but did not cede control of the volume knob. Austin bobbed his head in the backseat and hummed when he thought he knew the tune.

"So this was your little sister?" Vicki asked. "Why isn't she at Roselawn with Grandma and Grandpa?"

"Grandma and Grandpa didn't know they'd be at Roselawn yet, I suppose," Lorraine said. She knew this answer was incomplete. She'd given up on trying to find an explanation for her father's depositing the baby in unfamiliar ground so far away from the family's corner of the world, knowing that whatever the reason it couldn't have said anything good about her father. And she'd recently come to suspect that some truths were best left out of a family history. Otherwise, every shortcoming and all sorrows would carry forward from generation to generation.

"And nobody ever went out to visit the grave? They never even put in a headstone?"

"It was a long time ago," Lorraine said. "Things were different."

Vicki sat quietly for a few minutes before she said, "Wayne asked me to marry him. Again."

This news pleased Lorraine, for it must have meant that the baby was Wayne's, that he knew about the pregnancy, and that he was trying again to do right by Vicki and Austin. By doubting whether the baby was Wayne's, Lorraine had underestimated her daughter, but she didn't feel sorry for it. With her worst fears erased, she felt good. She had so often watched her daughter do the selfish and shortsighted thing that she learned to avoid letdowns by expecting the worst.

"What did you say this time?"

"Yes," Vicki said. "I said yes."

Lorraine could see her daughter looking in her direction, but try as she might, she couldn't contain herself. She smiled a broad, toothy smile—a smile so wide she knew it contorted her face and made her look like a child or a fool. She reached and patted Vicki's thigh, then squeezed her leg just above the knee. She said the news was delightful, that Jim would be delighted, just delighted.

"Oh, knock it off," Vicki replied. She smiled just as widely.

Lorraine had no trouble finding her way around in the cemetery this time, and when they climbed out of the station wagon, the late-morning sun struck them with a force that promised summer was near. She led the way as they walked to Row D, then along until they came upon the new grave marker. She noticed the places where the workers had patted the black soil against the freshly buried stone, a simple slab in a deep color of red.

"Here it is," Lorraine said. The three of them stood side-by-side and stared down at the stone, which bore the words "Baby Girl Anderson, Lost at Birth, September 10, 1955." Two figures of angels—plump and cherub-like—framed the text. The marker looked lovely—simple, dignified, respectful. Lorraine thought about her sister down there or up above or wherever she was, and she hoped this gesture—however overdue—might come as a comfort. She said, "Doesn't it look fine?"

"That's it?" Vicki asked.

"Sure," Lorraine replied. "That's all a person needs."

"I guess so," Vicki said, standing alongside her mother and holding Austin in place by resting her hands on his shoulders. "You ever think about how your life would have been different with her around?"

Lorraine said no, and it was mostly true. She had long felt for her sister the sort of longing she had for other things in life that she had wished for but never known—a father who was open-hearted, a husband who was generous, children who wanted her company more than anything else they could get from her. Her father would have believed this feeling—this ache for absent things—was a weakness, even a vice, but she forgave herself for it.

"I was a little kid at the time," she told Vicki, "and life went on."

Austin twisted away from his mother, dropped down close to the marble, and ran his fingertips along the grooves that formed an angel's face. His bare knees pressed into the wet grass, which was short and freshly green. He leaned in close and studied the crisp lines of the letters, as though he were trying to figure out how they had been made.

"Come on, Austin," Vicki said. "Get off of it."

Vicki bent to yank him back, but her mother reached out a hand and stopped her.

"Let him be," Lorraine said.

The two women stepped back as the boy stood up, brushed off his knees, and dashed away down the row, stomping on some markers and dodging others. He stopped at the waterspout and cranked it open. Water rushed downward, splashing onto his shoes and soaking the ground around him, and he clapped his hands as he danced away. Vicki laughed and shook her head. Lorraine stood and watched her grandson play and wished he'd never have to stop.

The
Deep
Route

Len picked up his son and, with time to kill, drove down to the park right by where the bridge had collapsed. Forever he had been trying to teach his kid how to catch a football, and on a blue June morning, even after a sleepless night, he could think of nothing better to do. The plan was they'd run a couple drills and work off some of the kid's energy while they waited until eleven o'clock. That's when Danielle could take her lunch and they'd all go for pancakes.

He and the kid could hardly find space to chuck a ball around because here and there hulked huge green girders—all bent, wrenched, and rusting away. Everything had been reeled out of the river nearly two years ago and the new bridge built. You could hear the freeway traffic's buzz, yet here were these metal bones nobody knew what to do with.

"What's that junk?" the kid asked as Len windmilled his throwing arm. They'd moved into some open grass on the downstream end of the park, a spot about the size of a rich guy's backyard or the whole infield of a real baseball diamond.

"That's nothing." Len didn't want the kid worrying about bridges falling down. "Run around a little. Get loose."

The kid kept staring at the girders, and as he trotted off, he aimed straight for them.

"Hey!" Len yelled. "I said keep away from there."

The kid circled into open grass—never looking at Len, pretending he hadn't heard. He had black hair like his mother's and wore a bright red T-shirt with huge letters spelling out the name of the store it came from, which was something Len couldn't stand. The kid zigzagged across the grass for no good reason, then charged toward the water like he'd just noticed it, like maybe he was making a discovery that'd be a huge wonder to them both. Len called his name and, when the kid kept going, tucked the ball into an elbow and ran after him. The kid had a huge lead but pulled up where the grass gave way to rocks and mud.

"Come on!" Len said as he thundered up and seized his son around the upper arm. "Let's focus!"

"Holy crap," his son said. "Can we swim here?"

"Nobody swims in the river," Len replied, but the question twirled his memory back to high school, when he and his best friend would hike down at nighttime and empty a backpack of beer right near here, where the Mississippi skulked through and separated the college buildings on either bluff. They thought it was cool how the dark, empty river bottoms interrupted the whole city, how hardly anybody seemed to notice, and how nobody went down there.

"How come?" the kid asked.

"How come what?" Len wanted to keep thinking about that old friend. He'd been a real cool guy, long-haired the way girls liked and five o'clock-shadowed from eighth grade on. It'd been slick, having a friend like that.

"How come we can't swim?" The kid shook loose of Len's grasp but moved close alongside him.

Smirking, Len said, "I had a friend who bet me fifty bucks I couldn't swim across."

"Could you?" The kid smiled up at him with eyes eager to admire. "Did you?"

The Deep Route

"You kidding?" Len smacked the football between his palms and bounced up onto the balls of his feet. "Let's get down to business. Come on now."

He jogged toward the center of the grassy area, a good distance back from the water. The kid followed, yipping more questions about the river, the bet, the swim. Len answered, "Focus! Time's short!"

Danielle worked at the hospital, where Len had cooked in the cafeteria until he'd gotten caught stealing a case of toilet paper from the storeroom. She was Len's girlfriend, not the kid's mother, which wasn't Len's idea of a super situation. The mother, Len's ex, was a hot-looking but hard-hearted girl he'd met when she was twenty-one, turning harder and meaner all the time now. He'd gotten tangled up with her long before he found Danielle, and he wished he could undo that without undoing the kid, wished he could do some time-traveling and pluck that little embryo right out of the mean one and tuck it into Danielle. He wouldn't change a thing about that kid, except maybe his hands. Eight years old and he still clapped at a football like a trained seal.

Len followed his usual routine. They began a few feet apart, underhand tossing the ball back and forth. After five catches in a row, they each took one big step backward and threw again. A dropped pass meant they'd start over. All the time Len kept talking, encouraging and congratulating, not barking directions and criticizing like every jackass coach he'd had as a kid.

"We welcome the ball," Len said. "Our hands make a soft landing spot."

"Uh-huh," the kid replied, staring at an incoming pass like it was a lightning bolt zapping down.

"The ball doesn't want to be squeezed." Len switched to overhand after ten straight passes. "Nobody wants to be grabbed. Nobody wants to be strangled."

He tried to put some air under the ball, to send it on a nice arc, but no matter what the kid still looked afraid. His mother kept his hair clipped tight on the sides, and Len could see all the little jaw muscles clench as each pass dropped in.

"We welcome it with soft hands." Len wished a coach had just once explained things to him this way. He'd wasted so much time having to figure it out on his own. "We ease it in."

Growing up, Len was always having to figure things out on his own. His dad left early, tuned out completely. Nobody moaned over it. Len never bitched, never considered what was missing. His mother tried to fill in, but there was a lot she didn't know. Making your hands soft? That was the least of it. Would've been nice to have someone around to tell him to pluck the creeping hairs between his eyebrows; that's what guys do, or ought to. Would've been nice to have someone around to tell him that wasn't herpes; that was jock itch and one hell of a case. Would've been nice to have someone around to tell him you don't say "I love you" to a girl just because she lets you take off her shirt; you'll disgust her and, anyway, that feeling you've got won't last. Len planned to make sure his kid knew what he needed to know.

Usually they played catch in the alley behind Len's apartment building. On good days they'd work it past twenty or twenty-five straight, with Len lofting neat spirals and the kid chucking his wounded ducks. Len figured that this time they'd practice awhile, pile back in the car, and go wait for Danielle outside the loading-dock door.

The kid kept dropping balls—ones Len knew were right on target—and the two of them started over, started over, and started over. They couldn't get to twenty. It went on so long that Len quit talking. He threw and threw, and when the drop came, he'd stomp back to the middle and begin again. When they finally got to nineteen, Len took a deep breath. After his long night of bartending and what-not afterward, he was so tired his joints ached. He kept in decent shape, didn't have any fat on him, but his body didn't endure like it used to.

"The ball is our baby," Len said. "We bring it home real gentle."

The Deep Route

He rainbowed a pass toward his son, who retreated three steps for some reason and had to hustle forward, coming in off-balance and stretching with eyes closed and arms rigid as steel. The pigskin slapped his palms and popped up. Len saw everything like slo-mo. The ball fluttered, glanced off the kid's forehead, and hit the dirt. The boy tumbled down too.

"Dang it!" the kid shouted. "I had that one!"

He stood up all happy and peppy to retrieve the ball.

"Here," he said. "I'll punt to you!"

"No," said Len, already walking back to start over. The kid booted a liner that flew over his head and bounced away.

"That's not what we do!" Len had to force out the *we* this time. It was something Danielle taught him, though he couldn't really remember the reasoning behind it, other than *we* sounding nicer than *you*. He walked over and grabbed the ball.

"Punt it back," the boy said. "It's funner."

Len didn't know what to say. He wasn't about to start kicking balls around like an idiot. He cocked his arm and gave the go-deep wave with his left hand. The kid didn't budge. Len waved again. Still nothing from the kid, so Len fired—a flat spiral with a tight spin, a total beauty. The kid barely got his hands up, and, whomp, it nailed him right on the nose.

The kid let out a yip, partly drowned out by the noise of cars on the new bridge, and staggered around like some wounded TV soldier before dropping onto his back. Len couldn't help but laugh. Getting whomped in the face hurt like hell, but watching someone get whomped in the face was something else. He jogged over and kneeled next to the kid, who had his hands over his face but wasn't crying yet.

"It's not funny!"

"I know," Len said.

"You're laughing!"

Len tried to deny it, but his voice broke up and he couldn't speak at all, could only flatten his grin and try to crunch up his brow in an a way that said *I care. I'm concerned.*

"You are!" the kid said. Then he started to bawl, and with the tears came bubbles of blood from both nostrils. Scowling, he rolled over, got to his knees, and stood unsteadily. Blood dripped onto his shirt and disappeared into the red fabric.

Len took him by the shoulder to get a good look at that nose, but the little guy spun away and took off running, bursting across the open field with blood and tears streaming back. He went straight for the junk from the old bridge, and Len had to chase him through a maze of banged and twisted girders, some of them taller than the kid and some taller than a grown man.

The kid's mother clickety-clacked down the hallway. Len knew it was her before she came into the waiting room, which was a narrow and oddly dim space with bare walls and a floor of peach-colored tile. The kid and Len and Danielle sat side-by-side in a row of chairs along the wall, but you wouldn't have known anyone was there except the kid and his mother. She totally ignored Len, went straight to the kid, bent over, baby-talked to him, and rubbed his back.

"Oh, Sweets, it'll be okay," she whispered. "You'll be okay."

Some nurse had stuffed cotton into the kid's nostrils and told them to wait for a doctor, who would do something about the busted nose, which had puffed and purpled but didn't look too far out of whack. At least Len didn't think it looked bad. He'd been glad no one else was waiting; it'd given him hope the kid might be patched up before his mother could get there. But things were never that easy.

"It was an accident," said Danielle, who leaned across Len and looked at the kid with elephant-mama eyes. She wore a kitchen uniform, although she'd been made a cafeteria manager and didn't have to. That's the sort of person she was. And even in the checkered pants and high-necked white top you'd recognize her as a cool girl, a rocker. She was twiggy and wore a lot of mascara. "They were playing football."

The kid's mother stiffened. She hardly looked like the person Len had married. But that was seven years ago now, the divorce six. She'd gone sort of doughy. The same girl was in there, the big-titted college chick Len met at the bar and accidentally knocked up. But her cheeks and her jaw and, from what Len could see through her snug office suit, the whole rest of her had grown two inches of dough.

"He's sorry," Danielle said.

Len's ex went on ignoring Danielle, which made him mad, made him shift around in his seat, made his face turn red. She could treat him like crap. That was nothing. But she couldn't do that to Danielle.

"Hey," Len said, "Danielle's talking to you."

His ex just went right on whispering to the kid, patting him, grasping his hand, and making sad faces. Finally she turned, still acting like Len was invisible, and frowned at Danielle.

"Sorry," the ex said, voice soft and eyes misty. She had a broad face, and way back when, Len thought she looked like she was always verging on a smile. He'd liked that, but he saw none of it now.

"It's not a real bad break," Danielle said. "He hit him almost straight on."

"Hit?" The ex's voice turned high, sharp.

"With the ball," Danielle replied.

"Don't act like you think I smacked him," Len said. "I already told you what happened."

Len knew he'd explained everything on the phone, explained it all very clearly. He'd explained how he was using his personal free time to get the kid some exercise, using his personal free time to teach the kid something a dad should teach a son. He didn't have to do it. He could've let the kid go off to his babysitter's like most days, but what kind of childhood was that?

"Move over," the ex said.

Len and Danielle slid down, and she took the chair next to the kid. He started bawling as soon as his mother put her arm around him and pulled him close. She cooed and kissed his head and choked up herself.

"You and that stupid football," she said to Len. "Give it up, would you?"

"He likes it," Len replied.

"He hates it."

Len looked at his kid, hoping he'd shake his head or speak up.

"Anyway, he needs to learn," Len said. "How's he going to have any friends if he can't even play catch worth shit?"

His ex let out a "ha" and said, "Because football players are noted for their true and loyal friendship? Because you made so many friends that way?"

"Oh, knock it off," Danielle said.

Len, his ex, and even the kid looked at her.

"You shouldn't fight," Danielle said. "Accidents happen, you know? They were playing catch. That's a good thing, right?"

The ex said nothing. They all sat back, and the only sound was the kid's whimper. Then, out of nowhere, the ex said, "You should know, Danielle, that he's full of crap."

Len got confused for a second, couldn't think of anything to say.

"Whatever he's told you, forget it," she went on. "He lies. He lies about everything."

"Aw, crap," Len said, turning toward Danielle and leaning his body between her and his ex. "Don't listen. She'll say anything."

Danielle looked at him, her face wide open, wondering.

"Ask him how long he actually played football," the ex said. "Ask him if he was ever really in a band."

Len mouthed the word *crazy*.

"Go ahead and ask him." She didn't raise her voice, didn't sound angry. She just talked coolly like some TV detective. "Ask him if he ever graduated from high school."

"Knock it off." Len watched Danielle, trying to figure her thoughts. "That's stupid."

"GED," his ex said. She pulled the kid against her chest, and half-whispered as if he wouldn't hear. "He was a loser with a GED who got a job bartending so he could hook up with college girls."

"You see why I left?" Len said to Danielle. "This is what—"

"He didn't leave." The ex cupped her hands over the kid's ears. "I kicked him out because he was still sticking it in anything that moved, even though he had a wife and baby."

Len felt like he might throw up. She didn't have to say this—not in front of the kid and not in front of Danielle, who'd been really kind and hadn't questioned his every decision and seemed to like going for pancakes with the kid whenever they could. He kept watching Danielle, and the weird thing was that she didn't look mad or sad or shocked or confused. She stared back with empty eyes, then blinked and leaned around him. She looked at the ex and the kid, then sat back and closed her eyes.

Len leaned back too, his shoulder rubbing against hers. He noticed how they didn't pipe music into the waiting room and wished they did. That would've helped. He could hear every breath from his ex and his girlfriend, every snort and swallow from his son.

Danielle's chair squeaked as she leaned and looked around him again.

"You know why he lost his job here?" she asked.

"Would you knock it off?" Len said. He'd given a cover story to his ex and kid after the toilet paper thing. The ex was always looking for a reason to make him suffer over visitation or child support. "We've got a wounded kid here. Where's a damn doctor?"

"He stole toilet paper," Danielle said. "They caught him on video. He took a whole huge box, ninety-six rolls."

Len went in by the back door, checked the calendar to make sure he wasn't scheduled, and goosed the new bartender on his way past. She yelped but smiled when she saw who was sneaking around behind the bar.

"Oh, sorry," Len said. "I thought you were someone else."

"Sure," she replied. "Happens all the time."

The room was dark, like always, and mostly empty. Two bouncers stood inside the main doors and kept busy bragging about who they'd nailed last night, or maybe arguing about the same thing. They gestured and flapped their big mouths, but Len couldn't hear them over the music, which was some old song from the jukebox. Foreigner or Foghat, he couldn't remember. He recognized it as one of those songs that people chose only because it was cool to play old songs and then sit back with friends and have a laugh. Lots of times, late at night, they'd even sing along. This time the chooser of the song must've been one of the college girls in the corner booth. They looked happy.

Len grabbed a plastic cup and scooped it full of ice.

"Why the long face?" the new bartender asked.

"You don't want to know," Len said.

He couldn't say why, but he liked this girl. Her hair was orange and skin pale. She wore her bangs long and straight so they hung in front of her eyes. She had a long nose. She was far from perfect, and he always forgot her name—but still liked her quite a lot. He wished he could think of her name. What was it? Marcy or Darcy? One of those.

"Sorry." She dipped her hand into the dish sink and pulled out a soapy glass. "Female trouble?"

"You could say that," Len replied, immediately regretting it and wishing he'd steered her another way. He didn't want her marking him as taken or knowing his baggage. He did some quick thinking. "Nothing big. It's just something that ended, you know, a while ago, but we're trying to still be friends."

She scrunched up her nose, then shrugged.

"I know." He shook his head and flashed a stupid-me smile. "Never works."

She nodded and said, "You know what? You should smile more."

Len got maybe one second to feel good before she abruptly shifted expression.

"What?" he said.

"Did you work last night?" she asked.

Len nodded.

"You closed?"

Len nodded again. The Thursday night crowd had trashed the place, meaning he'd cleaned until almost five in the morning and by that time there was no point in going home to bed because he had to pick up the kid at eight. He'd been exhausted, which was probably why he lost his cool and threw the ball so hard and whomped the kid, which eventually led to his ex-wife promising to see him in court and Danielle telling him to leave her alone. When she'd taken off from the waiting room, he'd followed through the hospital and toward her office. She finally pointed him into the dead-end hallway and told him she was a grown up, she had a job to do, she didn't want to talk to him, and she'd call if that ever changed.

It'd been rough, but Len felt okay now, after going for pancakes by himself and heading back to the apartment to crash.

"Better watch out," said Marcy or Darcy or whatever. "Sheila's pissed."

That Sheila—fat-assed, loudmouthed, and somehow his boss. He loathed her. He should've been her boss, should've been running the place by now, but things had gotten screwed up after the pregnancy. He'd met the ex at this very place, and for her he'd left a perfectly good life of free booze, nice girls, and no alarm clocks. He'd tried to get it right—to find a job with decent pay and daytime hours, to go home at night and play with his kid and love his wife—but it didn't stick. He'd botched things again and again right through to the hospital and the toilet paper and Danielle. He'd finally gone begging for his old job, the only one he'd ever liked, which brought him back to the bar, which put him where he could be barked at by the likes of Sheila.

"Pissed about what?" Len asked.

"Ladies' room," the new bartender said, crunching her nose again and squinting. "Barf all over."

"Fuck me," Len said. He hated cleaning the bathrooms. Nothing made you feel less human than wiping up the disgusting things peed, shat, puked, or otherwise discharged by perfect strangers. "In the ladies' room?"

"You can't skip the ladies', Len." Marcy or Darcy held up a bottle of Wild Turkey, and when he nodded, poured it over the ice in his cup. "When are you gonna learn?"

"Don't tell me you had to clean it," he said. He wondered if she had tattoos in unseen places—or piercings. He'd never been with anyone who had hidden body piercings. "Please don't tell me Sheila did it."

"Oh, no," said the new bartender, grinning. "It waits for you."

She checked to make sure the ladies' room was empty and gave him the go-ahead. He banged through the door, plastic cup of whiskey still in hand. The whole room stunk like vinegar and rotten beef. Strips of masking tape made an X over the doorframe on the end stall. He reached through and nudged the door open. There, a stew of misery. *This*, he thought, *must be a joke. Nobody could do this.*

Sheila sprang at him outside the ladies' room, finger wagging and her lips pursed sourly. When they'd first met Len sized her up as an aggressive loudmouth who'd been making and keeping friends through fear ever since grade school. Nothing yet changed his mind.

"Should've done it last night," she said. "Would've been easier when you were drunk."

"I wasn't drunk," Len said. She constantly accused him of getting drunk during his shifts, which he hardly ever did. "I must've missed it."

The Deep Route

Sheila chuckled and said, "You know where the mop is. Hope you got your own chisel."

Chin down, Len slipped past her and headed for the back room. The new bartender acted busy at the dish sink, pretending not to notice what Sheila was putting him through. He cut behind the bar, and there it was—the bottle of Wild Turkey—right on the end of a row, right on his way. He snatched it as he passed and braced for Sheila to start bitching. No one said a word. Then he felt he had no choice but to keep moving. He strode straight out the back door, stuffed the bottle under his shirt, and hustled to his car.

Dusk stretched on forever as he drove through the city, along the river, up the opposite bank, and around again. Danielle had gone home and had her dinner by now, he imagined, and she would only make him feel like shit if he showed up. The kid, he knew, was at home too, probably sad about how his nose hurt, how no kid shows were on TV, how he couldn't catch worth crap, and how his dad was mean. And his ex was probably sitting close on the couch, speaking in a soft voice, and saying how it was all Len's fault and don't worry about having to see him anytime soon. When darkness finally came, he drove through the neighborhood where all the college girls lived. He could see some, drinks in hand, on front porches of the rundown rental houses. With his windows down, he could hear their laughter and loud talk. They were so brash, young girls. He sort of liked that.

After nightfall he felt safer sipping from the bottle as he drove. He crossed the new bridge—that wide expanse of white concrete, that huge thing that looked like nothing—and thought about his kid and the football and how things had gone wrong. He thought about how everything had always gone wrong, how he'd never been any good at sports, never any good with a guitar, never any good at anything but making girls feel important. He'd figured out that trick, eventually, but there was no call for passing his skill to an eight-year-old. What good was it, anyway? None of his girlfriends wanted him now. The only woman he might've had a shot with was that new bartender, and he couldn't go back there—not tonight, maybe not ever.

He speed-dialed the bar on his cell and waited ten rings before someone picked up.

"Who is this?" he asked.

"What?" A woman's voice answered back, a friendly voice like the new bartender's. The jukebox wailed in the background. "Hello?"

"It's Len," he half-shouted. He recognized the song. Journey, he was pretty sure. "Who is this?"

"Len? Where are you?"

"Who is this?" If she'd just say it, he wouldn't forget again. "Speak up."

"I can't hear," she answered. "Get your ass back to the bar."

She hung up.

Len cornered onto a road hooking down to the riverside and headed into the park where he'd taken the kid. His car swooped across the parking lot, a small rectangle of blacktop dotted near its center by widely spaced lights emitting a dull orange glow. After parking in the corner nearest the girders and patch of open grass, he dialed the bar again, but no one was picking up. He let it ring until he got a recording and the line went dead. He drank more from the bottle, waited two minutes, and tried once more. Sheila answered. He clapped the phone closed, tucked it into his pocket, and swore.

Alone and without hope of changing that fact, Len slumped against his seat and closed his eyes. He rested, awash in his day's regrets and desires. He realized the muscles of his shoulders and neck were locked up, had been forever. He relaxed them. He retreated into his thoughts. He'd arrived at this place before—this messed-up mental intersection. His experience helped him to consider his hopes and pangs with a kind of detachment he believed was a symptom of maturity. Like before, Len hungered for a new life and a new girl, a clean sheet upon which he could rewrite his story and an unknown body that could work for him in ways familiar things never can. But, more than even the girl, he longed to *do* something tonight—something a little crazy.

This urge made him smile. He'd first gotten to know it when he was nineteen, after powering through one of those parties that boil into utter wantonness, when lust and aggression, flat beer and cheap drugs flood through a place and everyone ends up breathless and tangled on the floor with near-strangers or alone and gasping as their bodies exorcise foul things from deep down. The night had gone on and on, and finally with dawn not far off he'd risen from the kitchen floor where he'd been belly-stuck to a chubby girl called Katrina—a name he'd never forget though it belonged to a person he'd never speak to again—and walked out into the gray light of the backyard. He'd stood naked in the dew-damp grass, looking at the dark windows of neighboring rental houses, and smiled as he pissed into the wide open. Then, wanting only to try something new and wild, he'd dashed off through unfamiliar yards and unlit alleyways. He hadn't wanted to be seen, had in fact hidden against a hedge when a crappy car cornered from a cross street and rattled past. He'd streaked his way home, hadn't been discovered, and hadn't told a soul. And, once over the shock of his own weirdness, he'd felt revived.

More than a decade evaporated since that night. He'd gone through girls and jobs, other girls and other jobs. He'd even gone through a marriage and the unplanned arrival of fatherhood. He hadn't once felt another urge to run around naked, but in lost hours of other explosive nights he'd sped northbound across half a mile of southbound freeway, he'd scaled the fence at a city zoo and lobbed marshmallows at the brown bears, and he'd heaved an empty Bud bottle against the picture window of a house belonging to a couple who had once been his mother and father in-law. Each time involved risk and fear, and each reinforced a notion in him that he had exceptional nerve, which made him different, which distanced him from the droning mainstream.

To Len, this was obvious: He'd have to swim that river. He'd win the bet with his old pal, wherever he was, and he'd do another thing that others wouldn't. He'd do it by himself, tell no one. He pulled the door latch and swung his feet onto the asphalt. Moving toward the river, Len veered along the flank of the girders. He got close and ran his fingers up one's edge, smooth against his touch but hourglass warped. He climbed on top and walked it like a giant balance beam. The blue-white glow of lights on the new bridge hovered over the girders and the grass, and reflected on the river's shivering surface. Traffic buzzed on.

Len jumped down and sat with his back against the steel. He envisioned the swim, preparing so he wouldn't give up, wouldn't panic, and wouldn't sink like a chunk of concrete. The water would be cold; it would take his breath when he jumped in. But he'd swim hard into it, and soon he'd adjust. (This was another thing he'd had to figure out for himself: You only suffer when you stand around in cold water and wait to get used to it. If you dive in and swim hard for thirty seconds, any water feels fine.) He was pretty sure he'd make it.

He rested and thought about his high-school friend and the times they'd had down along the river. They were always talking and daring each other and never doing anything. They always said they'd found the perfect place to bring chicks, and even now Len figured maybe he should bring a girl down there sometime, maybe that new bartender. She was worth one more try.

He stood, pulled his phone from the pocket of his jeans, and tapped to redial. This time she answered right away.

The Deep Route

"Marcy," he said. Bar noise roiled through his earpiece. He could hear the mix of competing voices and, above them all, some weird old song. Len wasn't sure, but he thought it was Eddie Money. "This is Len."

"What?" she said. "I can't hear."

"Darcy!" He shouted, hoping to be right. "It's Len!"

"Hey, you asshole! Where are you?"

"Nowhere."

"What?" She spoke quickly, her voice coming through high and happy. "Just get back here, okay?"

"I can't, can I?" He plugged his free ear and hunched his shoulders. "What about Sheila?"

"I covered you." The new girl gave a little laugh, like she'd let him in on a joke. "I cleaned it, okay? It's done."

Some sudden heat surged through Len. His ears hummed. He stood there blinking, lips open.

"Just get back here!" She hung up again.

Len looked toward the river, then turned and started toward his car and the orange glow of the parking lot. He broke into a jog. "Darcy," he said to himself. "Darcy." He fired up the car and steered back along the curving park road and into the brightness of the city. With his window down and cool air coming in, Len gave it gas and sped into an opening between pulses of traffic. The hiss-hum of rubber on concrete blended with a tired tune playing on his radio. It was something by Bob Seger. Len sang along. He knew the song but couldn't name it.

And
Other
Delights

Two o'clock in the afternoon and there he is, my grandson, licking Cool Whip from the bellybutton of his latest girlfriend. I'm talking broad daylight here, front porch of our lake place. God knows what they do after dark. And there she is, mostly undressed and spread across the old sofa, twitching and giggling so I know whatever he's doing with that tongue of his tickles something fierce. And here I am on the top step, watching through a rusted screen, seeing things I shouldn't see, my bladder ready to burst and my hands coated in grease from the broken-down outboard I've tinkered with all day.

I tiptoe away from the door, hoping to Christ they don't hear me. I ought to be able to take a leak outside—we're in the country, after all—but the next-door kids are playing in the yard. The basement is my only choice.

I ease open the cellar door, whose hinges howl anyways, step down into the darkness, and feel around for the string that hangs from the light above the wash tub. I search for an empty container—an ice-cream bucket, a milk bottle, a pot to piss in. When the situation gets desperate, I unzip, lean over the basin, and let 'er rip.

I never imagined this would happen to my body, this physical backtracking toward helplessness, a sort of return to infancy. This urge used to come on gradually, with plenty of notice. Now my bladder is a dry riverbed one minute and a bursting dam the next. And where does it end?

At the pharmacy, I suppose, taking that long walk toward the register, a package of Depends tucked under my arm. I can hardly bear to think of that.

But I'm feeling okay now. In fact, I could stand here all day, breathing in the cool air and doing my business. Nobody comes downstairs anymore, not since Marie passed, and nobody knows or worries much what I do with myself.

I hear footsteps as I tuck in, first her quiet prance across the floor overhead, toward the bathroom, and next his clumsy stomp, stomp, stomp, followed by the slam of the storm door. I run a little water into the sink, then head back up the steps and into the sunshine. My grandson rounds the corner of the cabin as I let the cellar doors clash to a close.

"Hey, Gramps." He huffs his words—still winded, I assume, from what was going on inside. "That you making all that noise?"

"What noise?"

"We heard someone in the cellar. Thought maybe we were getting robbed."

"Not much to steal down there," I say. "But good to know you're on top of things."

Tuck—short for Tucker—stares at me hard and puckers his lips like a grade-schooler trying to decipher a math problem. He's twenty-two now, and sarcasm is still too much for him. Always been that way. Good thing he's handsome. Good thing he doesn't resemble the long-faced, soft-chinned Irish on our side. Good thing he inherited his father's square jaw, clear eyes, and thick brown hair, which he chooses to comb only on Christmas and Easter, also the two days he makes it to Mass.

Fashion is the folly of youth, my wife used to say, but I don't understand why anybody would want to walk around looking like he spent the night in the drunk tank. Tuck wears only his swim trunks, enormous yellow things that stretch down below his kneecaps. Swirls of his hair aim off in all directions, and a patch near his forehead looks to be matted with a certain white substance—the Cool Whip I had planned to use to mix a bowl of Marie's fruit salad. He finally shrugs.

"You know it, Gramps. I've always got my eyes open."

"I'd better get back to the boathouse," I say. "Your folks will be disappointed if the pontoon's not seaworthy by the time they get here."

"Just Mom," he says.

"What's that?"

"You said my *folks*." He looks at his bare feet. "My dad's not coming. Obviously."

"A slip," I say. They signed the divorce papers two years ago, which was six months or so after we buried Marie, but their marriage was over long before. "I hadn't forgotten."

Tuck's shoulders slump, and he drags his big toe in the dirt. A second ago I'm having a little fun and he's all high off love and whipped cream, and now he's forlorn. The kid is so soft. I shouldn't forget that.

"I could probably use your help," I say, "if you're not too busy. What are you lovebirds doing inside on an afternoon like this anyways?"

"Nothing much." He looks over his shoulder toward the smoked glass of the bathroom window. "Just having a snack."

"Anything left for me? I could stand something to eat right about now."

"I'm afraid not." He can't help but grin. Then he straightens up and claps his hands. "Let's get after that Mercury. What's wrong with it this year?"

He's being a smart aleck, but he's dead right. The Mercury is an annual headache and fixing it is as much a tradition as our Fourth of July picnic. It's an old twenty-five horse we bought used, along with the pontoon boat, during Tuck's third or fourth summer at the cabin.

Marie said our kids weren't interested in water-skiing anymore—they'd grown by then—and the grandkids, Tuck was the first, were far too young. "We need something safe, sort of a pleasure craft," she said, "not a speedboat." So we sold the runabout and bought the biggest, ugliest pontoon I'd ever seen. Marie loved its sturdy railings, which would keep the babies safe, and its broad canopy, which would keep her fair skin out of the sun. I wrote the check, and two days later I was taking apart the Mercury for the first time.

Most of me hopes this year will be the last, that I'll never have to listen to that thing spit and rattle again. I don't mind the work. It's usually pretty simple—clean out the carburetor, replace the spark plugs, that sort of thing. I've learned my way around that motor pretty well by now, and I just keep it mounted on a sawhorse in the boathouse until it's fixed and running smooth—relatively smooth anyway. But the whole production seems mostly pointless now.

The kids and grandkids come up for the Fourth like always, but nobody has much fun. Everyone sits around real quiet all day, and then after supper, we skulk onto the pontoon and circle the lake, all of us thinking about how Marie loved trolling along the shore and playing tour guide: "The brown one is the Pearsons' old place; they paid eighteen thousand years ago and just sold for a quarter million; and the yellow cabin, (that's starting to look rundown, too bad), well, that still belongs to the Lundgrens; he's the office supply man from Minneapolis." She'd go on and on, and the kids, even the little ones who couldn't have cared less, would lean back on their bench or their lawn chair or their mom's lap and listen good. I'd steer wherever she pointed.

Tuck drove up a day early to help me get ready, sent by his mother because last year I didn't have any eggs in the fridge, hamburger in the freezer, or sheets on the beds when she showed up. The first summer—the holiday came only three months after the funeral—I knocked myself out to make everything perfect, mainly for the sake of the grandkids. But last year I figured people would expect to pitch in, which they ought to have done years ago instead of treating their mother like a housemaid. Anyhow, I'm glad Tuck is here. He can do the heavy lifting when we haul the motor down to the dock, then wade in and help me get the Mercury mounted.

He stands waist deep in green water when I ask about the girl he has brought along, without my okay, and, I suspect, without the permission of his mother.

"So where'd you meet this April?"

"Autumn," he says.

"Come again?"

"Her name's Autumn, Gramps." He sets the motor in place and steadies it there with one hand while he uses the other to yank at a coil of seaweed brushing against his back. "I met her at school, in a speech class, which I hated."

"That so?" I kneel at the back of the pontoon's deck and lean through the narrow gate that keeps the tykes away from the gas tank and the motor.

"She was brilliant at it, though," Tuck says. "She's brilliant at everything."

"Sounds like a good catch." I crank on the nuts that clamp the Mercury in place. "Sure you're up to the job?"

He looks at me with his huge, wet puppy dogs and his eyebrows arched halfway up his forehead.

"Jeez, kid," I say. "Haven't you learned to take a joke yet? All you got to do is laugh and give it right back."

Tuck shows me his aw-shucks smile. He can't give it back, I can tell. The kid still doesn't know how give a guy the needle. He's probably working on it, trying real hard to think of something sharp to say, but he pretends to be caught up in his work, which isn't much more than standing there and making sure I don't fall out of the boat.

"I can't believe this thing still works," Tuck says. "It's almost as old as I am."

"Older," I reply. "But it's good for one more summer."

He smiles. "Don't tell me you're finally going to buy a new motor."

"Not exactly."

Tuck looks up when he hears his girlfriend—Autumn, not April—whistle from the cabin. She stands with one foot inside the porch, the other on the front step, and the screen door propped against her back. Our cabin, a little one-and-a-half story with cedar shakes the weather has turned gray, sits on the top of a steep slope, looking down on our dock and the weedy, washed-out shoreline that passes for a swimming beach. There's a flat spot right along the water's edge where a gravel road once ran, before the county put in a new highway on the backside of the lake cabins, and a narrow set of forty-eight concrete steps climbs to the front door.

"Chow time!" Autumn hollers.

She has been good enough to cook for the three of us, and when Tuck and I plop down at the kitchen table, she sets out our plates, each piled high with Kraft dinner, and pours three tall glasses of milk. She wears only her little bikini top and some cut-off blue jeans, and she has pulled her hair up in a ponytail. The girl has perfect skin, soft and clear with a little glow below her eyes. She's put together like somebody who comes from good stock, Italian or maybe part Spanish, not like the slouching Scandinavians and chubby German girls I knew in school.

"This is a tasty dish, Autumn," I say. "What do you call it?"

Tucker moans. "Gramps, come on. It's mac and cheese."

"That so?" I lift my glass and eye it carefully. "And what do you call this white beverage?"

He looks at me like I've come unhinged.

"Jokes, kid. Those are jokes," I say. "Just tweaking your girlfriend about her ambitious work in the kitchen."

"Duh." Autumn smiles at me. "Don't be a twit, Tuck."

It's hard for a man to keep his eyes to himself around a girl like Autumn, although I have already seen more of her assets than I've any right to. At my age, I don't stare or daydream the way a younger man might, but I still look. I appreciate her the way I do a clear sunrise.

"He's a little slow." Autumn sits down across from me. "Sarcasm, subtlety, irony—they're lost on him. I like to think it's because he's pure of heart."

"That's kind," I say.

Tuck shovels a forkful into his mouth and grins as he chomps away.

"But I suppose you're right," I say. "We shouldn't get after him for being innocent."

I worry about the kid; he seems too simple to get along in the world nowadays. I mean that in the old sense—simple, as in straight, honest, and forthright. Maybe Autumn has it right; he's just got a pure heart. But her choice of words makes me think about my days in school and what the nuns might have said about the goings-on earlier in the porch. Acts just don't come much more impure than that.

I almost wish I hadn't seen it, the way he licked up swirls of Cool Whip as his mouth traveled southward over the smooth skin above the waistline of her bikini. My God, that bikini, nothing but scraps of material made to cover the least amount of territory the law will allow, all of it held together by limp strings tied on her hips, between the ridges of her shoulder blades, at the base of her neck. And the color. Orange. Blaze orange. A color *intended* to attract the eye. When Marie and I took our honeymoon in Key West, she brought along an enormous bathing suit, one piece of industrial-strength fabric designed to correct some shortcomings and to obscure everything a woman had to offer. She looked fine that way.

Before we finish up, I grab a notepad from the junk drawer and jot down some chores that need finishing by the time the rest of the family arrives tomorrow. I put Autumn in charge of dusting up and getting sheets on all the beds in the loft, which is what the kids call the slope-ceilinged second floor. Over the years we have managed to cram in five twin beds and a cot I found at the army surplus store back in St. Paul. I tell Tuck to mow the front grass and to rake the weeds out of the water around the dock. I promise them we'll take the pontoon for a test run later on, and then I hit them with the good part.

"One other thing, Autumn," I say. "I need you to mix up a batch of fruit salad like Tuck's grandmother used to make. Nothing to it. Just strain the juice out of a couple cans of fruit cocktail, dump it in a bowl with a bag of those mini marshmallows, and mix it all together with a thing of Cool Whip. You'll find everything you need here."

She looks at Tuck, bites her lip, and nods. He stares at his empty plate.

"Nasty stuff," I say. "Too sweet for me, but the kids like it."

Autumn suddenly seems small, with her arms folded across her chest like she's caught a chill, and Tuck won't look at me, at her, at anything other than the tabletop. Finally, he stands, walks to the living room, and looks out at the front lawn.

"The grass doesn't look too long, Gramps."

"Then your job will be that much easier," I say.

It's no picnic, cutting the front lawn; it's even a bit dangerous. You have to push the mower back and forth across forty feet of hillside. The pitch is steep enough to make the Toro want to roll over, or to make a guy's feet slip from under him. I'd rather do just about anything else, and I figure that's why the Lord gave me a grandson.

"Okay," Tuck says. "I'll just get it over with."

He heads out to the porch and I shout after him.

"I hope you're not planning to cut the grass in those flip-flops."

He never answers. I shake my head. Autumn shrugs and smiles. Then she turns on the tap and leaves water running into the sink as she collects our dishes from the table. I offer to dry, but she says that's okay, she'll be fine alone. She gets right to work, taking a peculiar stance at the sink, her feet spread wide, like a first-timer on water skis, and her hips thrust against the countertop. She moves quickly—dip, scrub, rinse, dip, scrub, rinse. No way Marie would have allowed such a thing when she was around.

I become mesmerized watching this girl do her thing, and I get to daydreaming about other summer afternoons passed in this kitchen. The reason I bought the cabin was to give us all a break, a place where we could enjoy ourselves together, but Marie turned it into a chore. She cooked and cleaned and looked after kids all the time, even more than back home. I once told her to quit being the activities director and have some fun. She told me to mind my own business.

Autumn looks over her shoulder and sees me watching her, but she goes on working like before. I tell her she doesn't look very comfortable standing that way. She says I couldn't be more wrong. She's quite comfortable, and her back won't be sore afterwards.

"Sorry, I know it's not very ladylike." She pauses, holding a plate under the tap, and cocks her head. "Whatever that means."

"Who knows?" I say.

She doesn't seem to mind me being there, so I stay. I grab a can of root beer from the fridge, sit back down, and pretend to look over my to-do list. I keep thinking about Marie, but not as the mother and grandmother who sweated away summer days in this kitchen. I think about Marie when she was about Autumn's age, maybe a little younger, back around the time we got engaged.

Marie may have dressed in simple, modest clothes and lived a simple, modest life, but she wasn't a dull girl. I was lucky to find someone with that certain hunger. Even thirteen years with the nuns at St. Agnes couldn't squeeze it out of her. And it had a lot to do with why we got engaged when we did. Very young. Marie wanted things that way. Get married, be free, do what we liked, have a lot less to say at confession. She was eighteen, three weeks out of high school, when I proposed. I was twenty.

Her parents invited me over for dinner the Sunday after I gave Marie the ring. I never thought they cared for me much, but things were different that night. It was summer and hot like today. Still, everyone seemed cheery and optimistic, even Mr. O'Keefe, who was not a happy-go-lucky sort. Mrs. O'Keefe cooked up the standard Sunday dinner—pot roast, potatoes, canned corn. And once we'd finished, we sat around the table and made plans for the wedding.

Marie got up to clear our dishes, leaving me with her parents. Mr. O'Keefe lit up a cigarette. He was a serious smoker, the type with dark eyes and gray wrinkles on his face, though he was still a young man. Mrs. O'Keefe kept on talking—listing off who we'd invite, where we'd have the reception, and who'd be in the wedding party. She was a busybody, a small thing who was always talking, always planning something. Mr. O'Keefe and I listened and nodded and listened some more. Marie took away an armload of empty plates, set them in the sink, and watched from the kitchen. Then, when she was sure her parents weren't looking but I was, she lifted her skirt.

Before I could really understand what I was seeing, which was all pale skin and dark shadows, Marie smoothed her skirt back in place, smiled real big, and walked into the dining room. At that moment, I believed she was the perfect girl. I'd been foolish, always concentrating on her shortcomings—she wasn't tall enough or thin enough or built well enough—and figuring she was lucky to have me. But that night I saw things going on behind her tight grin, which I had thought to be unspectacular, and her brown eyes, which I had thought to be plain, and I knew I was the lucky one.

"I'm going to run into town," Autumn says. She has finished the dishes while I've been lost in thought. They drip dry in the rack. "Could you tell Tuck I'll be back in a little while?"

I straighten up and try to look like I've been focused on my list. I tap the pencil on the paper.

"What for?" I ask. "You don't want to waste an evening like this in town, do you? Not much going on in Aitkin."

She says she needs to pick up a thing or two and won't be gone more than an hour. Then she pulls the garbage pail from beneath the sink and double-knots the top of the bag, which is nowhere near full.

"All right then," I say. "I'll go ahead and make the fruit salad while you're out. Then you'll have one less thing to worry about."

"No, no." She looks out toward the porch, then back at me. "I'd like to do it. Leave it to me."

"All right, then," I say.

She slides into her sandals, slings her purse over her shoulder, and walks out. I hear her drop the garbage bag into the barrel on her way to Tuck's car. As she drives off, I wonder what the people in town will think of her when she, a total stranger, walks into the SuperValu wearing that bikini top, picks up a jumbo container of Cool Whip, and joins the line at the register.

Probably won't faze anybody. People do what they want these days.

An hour or so later I wake up on the sofa in the living room as the mower roars beneath the front window, then sputters to a stop. Tuck swings in through the porch door. His shoulders are pink and slick with sweat. He wears his yellow trunks and a pair of my snow boots, which had been gathering dust on a shelf in the boathouse.

"Some interesting footwear you've got there," I say.

"Safety first, Gramps." He looks pleased with himself. "What do you got for a thirsty boy?"

"Root beer's in the fridge."

He tromps off to the kitchen, clatters around in the Frigidaire, slams it closed, and snaps open a can of soda. I hear him chugging away, then a soft belch.

"Where's Autumn?" He leans in the doorframe and looks down at me.

"Gone to town," I say. "Grocery shopping."

He retreats into the kitchen.

"Come on," I say. "Let's get that pontoon out on the water."

The Mercury fires up and seems to be running fine as Tuck pushes us from the dock. I back out, steer toward the center of the lake, and pull back on the throttle until it's opened up all the way. The motor sounds good. When I let Tuck take over the wheel, he turns onto a line parallel with shore. I lean back on one of the benches at the front of the boat and watch the cabins go by, recalling the story of each one and the families that have spent summers there. They come and go—the people do. Some of them get divorced, sell off their lake homes, yank each other apart at the seams. Some grow old, die quietly, let their kids fight over who gets the place or how to divvy the profits when they sell. Some just decide the lake is too much work and go back to their weeklong stays at resorts where everything is taken care of. I still don't know what will become of our place and our family now that Marie is gone. I wish I could be rid of the work and the trouble and all the reminders, but then there's Tuck, sitting in the little captain's chair, guiding his craft, looking happy.

I ask him to circle back, and when we're about 100 feet off our beach, I tell him to cut the engine. We sit in silence for a moment or two.

"What's wrong?"

"Nothing," I say. "I just want to talk."

He chuckles like maybe I'm being sarcastic but stops when I don't smile in return.

"Really?"

"Listen, Tuck," I say. "I'm going to say some things you might not like, but just listen."

He nods.

"I hate that Mercury, and I hate this boat," I say. "I hate the weeds that grow around the dock, and I hate that damn hill. I hate the way the water tastes up here, and I hate the way that septic tank is always backing up. I'd like to be rid of it all."

Tuck looks stricken.

"I'd like to, but I can't," I say. "That's the truth. I want you to know the truth about your grandfather, to know that life doesn't get simple when you get old."

He nods again.

"Now," I say. "I figure you'd like me to keep this cabin forever. I suppose you have lots of happy recollections of times here, times when your grandma was looking out for you, times when even your mom and dad could smile a little and be kind to each other."

Tuck stares toward shore, so I keep talking.

"That's what we'll do. We'll keep this place, as long as that's what you want."

He's still got nothing to say.

"Tell me something, now," I say. "What are your plans with that girl?"

"Come on, Gramps." His voice quivers. "We're just hanging out."

"Is that what they call it now? Hanging out?" I ask. "Because it sure looked like something more than that was going on in the porch, and all that *hanging out* cost me two dollars' worth of Cool Whip."

Tuck's face turns bright red. He fidgets with the throttle, then turns the key to fire the motor.

"Sorry," he says, half shouting. He gives it gas and heads for the dock.

I stand up, push the throttle into neutral, and point for him to clear out of the chair. Once he sits down on the bench, I lay it out for him, talking just loud enough for him to hear me over the mumble of the outboard.

"Listen," I say. "Don't waste your time waiting around for something to hit you over the head, some signal from God telling you what to do with your life. You meet a girl like that, you better grab on while you can. Don't let her think twice."

"Jeez, Gramps." Tuck pouts, chin on chest. "You sure don't think much of me."

"Don't misunderstand," I say. "I'm talking about life here. You have to grab things when you can. Take chances. So what if it doesn't work out later? Your parents took a chance, and they ended up divorced. So big deal. There were good times. And there was you."

He looks wounded again.

"One last thing," I say. "You should know the truth about your grandmother."

Tuck glares at me and shakes his head.

"The first night we were here together, the two of us went skinny-dipping."

"Holy crap!" He buries his face in his hands. "I don't want to hear this."

"It was the best time we ever had at the lake," I say. "And we should have done it more."

I pull back on the throttle and head for the dock. Tuck smiles, laughs, and shakes his head. He rubs his eyes like he's trying to clear away an unpleasant vision, and he laughs more.

We tie up and climb the steps to the cabin, where Autumn holds a strainer full of fruit cocktail over the sink when we walk into the kitchen. Tuck grabs a spoon from the drawer, scoops out a heap of Cool Whip, and slurps it into his mouth. She punches him solid on the shoulder.

"Don't be a pig," she says.

I take a spoon and do the same. Soon the three of us sit around the table, sharing the tub of Cool Whip, eating it bite by bite until the container is scraped clean. I volunteer to head into town for more, so Autumn can mix the fruit salad.

"Not necessary," she says. "I bought extra."

I should have known.

Later that night, long after dark, I lie in bed reading through one of Marie's old paperbacks, one of the potboilers she loved so much, when I hear footsteps overhead. I put down the book, click off the lamp, and listen as Tuck and Autumn tiptoe down the stairs and squeak out through the porch door. One splash, then another, then water lapping on the shore.

Not Funny

Kent was only joking about the airplane. He meant nothing by it. He'd been leaning over the stove one morning, nudging some sausage links around a frying pan and half-ignoring Lori while she read aloud the day's most grabbing bit of news. She seemed happiest at breakfast time, when she'd sit behind an open laptop and begin the day with fresh news to dismay her, coffee steaming in her mug, and her body warm and free beneath a heavy bathrobe. Normally she'd scan the local paper's site before clicking over to the big Minneapolis one, where without fail she could find a story to disgust her, befuddle her, or otherwise compel her to moan, "For God's sake, listen to this." But that morning, the day Kent made his joke, she never got past the top feature from *The Daily Eagle*.

The juicy material came under the headline "New Business Will Pamper Your Pup." Lori quoted the story at length: "The Spaw will offer a full range of services to Southeastern Minnesota's canines, with everything from doggie daycare to puppy pedicures. Owner Duane Ubel sees a growing need for his services. 'Life is hectic nowadays,' he said. 'Two-career households put a lot of stress on dogs, and the owners want to do something special for their pets. We can care for these dogs and relieve owners of some of that guilt we all feel.'"

"Oh, yeah, we *all* feel that terrible, terrible guilt," Lori said. She sometimes interrupted her reading to make sarcastic comments. "You feel it, don't you, hon?"

Kent nodded as he worked at balancing the links on their sides, hoping to equalize the browning all the way around, a task requiring careful attention. The recitation of the news story continued with Lori groaning between paragraphs about the state-of-the-art grooming facilities, individual doggy suites with flat screen TVs and webcams, indoor play area with well-padded synthetic turf, and one-acre lawn with artificial fire hydrants.

"Man," Kent said, mainly because he'd lost interest and wanted to cut her off. "That's ridiculous."

"It's obscene," Lori said. "Completely obscene."

"Yeah," he replied. "Somebody ought to crash a plane into that place."

A wind of laughter caught in Lori's throat. A horror to kid about, she knew, but so much time had passed and so much had been said, mostly for fear and foolishness. What did it matter now? She laughed good and hard, and it felt like relief.

Barry Swanum hunched over the microphone as he read the seven o'clock news update, most of which he'd gleaned from that morning's edition of *The Daily Eagle*. There was a time when the radio station had its own reporters, but those days were long gone. Now he built a newscast from the wire and his own condensed and slightly reworded versions of top stories from the local paper, which he'd noticed wasn't what it used to be either.

"And finally today there's news from the city council," he said. "Attendance at the city pool fell short of the target this year, which may force an increase in fees next year. The council will take up the issue again sometime before opening day next summer. They've got plenty of time."

He paused and sipped from his coffee—allowing a short slurping sound into the microphone, a signature move of his—before continuing.

"It's fifty-one degrees at the moment, another glorious morning. Enjoy it while you can. Won't be long till snow flies." He chuckled. "This is the Bear coming to you from the Bear's Den. Here's something from the Beach Boys to give you a smile on the first day of autumn."

As the slow and sweet sounds of "Surfer Girl" eased across the airwaves, Barry clicked off his mike, removed his headphones, and went to take a leak. There wasn't much time, but he wasn't one to get flustered. A radio show was like a river: It just kept on flowing—rocky or smooth, swift or slow. One segment might be rough, but the next could as easily be perfect.

Thirty years in local radio had taught him a couple things: A good nickname went a long way, and he had that. And, more importantly, nothing could fuel a show better than homegrown oddities and controversies.

Yesterday had yielded an atypical one. The newspaper printed a brief about an eighteen-year-old ticketed for underage consumption of alcohol. When stopped by police, he denied drinking but confessed, "I just made out with a drunk girl." Barry read the item, suggested that the offender deserved points for creativity, and paused to laugh dryly. In lesser hands, this was merely a good chuckle, but Barry knew how to make something of it. He invited listeners to call and share the worst excuses they'd ever heard. The remainder of the show practically piloted itself, and it was, Barry knew, good radio.

Today's talker would come from the "Letters to the Editor" section of *The Daily Eagle*. A woman had written that the new "pet spa" in town stood as a symbol of American gluttony, that it explained why much of the world loathed Americans, that maybe somebody should "crash a plane into that place." Tailor-made for the Bear. All he had to do was read the letter, offer his tsk-tsk, and watch the phone lines light up.

"I saw a curious item in the paper today," Barry said when the music went down. "A local woman wrote in to criticize The Spaw, a new pet-care business over on Highway 14, and—here's the odd part—she seems to suggest The Spaw deserves to be a target for the terrorists."

He read the letter in its entirety—a lean five sentences, just right—and tacked on his commentary. "If that's a joke, I don't see what's funny," he said. (Another lesson: Keep it understated. No need for vitriol from the host. Let the callers handle that.) "I don't know about you folks, but I don't see anything humorous about September 11. To poke fun at such tragedy . . . well, it's just not funny at all."

Lori worked in a small office—a two-room suite on the third floor of an old school building downtown, next door to a dentist and across the hall from a family counseling office that always seemed to be empty. Paige, the serious and matronly woman who'd convinced Lori to leave the Twin Cities and move down to Rochester for this job, said only one thing the day the letter appeared: "Oh, honey, what on earth were you thinking?" Then she retreated to her office with a box of low-fat snack bars.

An empty desk sat alongside Lori's. That's where they stationed the intern, when they had one, which they didn't. Otherwise, it was just Paige and Lori—all day, every day. They couldn't ignore each other if they wanted to. At least that's what Lori had thought. Paige had done pretty well with silence and avoidance for two days.

"Can we sit down together this afternoon?" Lori finally asked. "I've got the city council meeting in Dodge Center tomorrow."

"I think you'd better let me handle that one," Paige said.

"What? Why wouldn't you send me?" Public meetings were Lori's turf. That part of their work—the communicating with and cajoling of public officials—was, in fact, the only concrete and easily definable part of her job description. The rest of it consisted mostly of fuzzy language about building coalitions, enhancing community collaboration, fostering public-private cooperation, and likewise. But going to city council meetings and pleading for money for low-rent apartment buildings, that was the one thing Lori knew for sure was hers. And she'd already put in a lot of work in Dodge Center, a little town nearby where a decade ago the migrant workers were made to sleep in tents or chicken coops or under the stars and where some were choosing, God knows why, to stick around and try to make a life on a farmhand's pay.

Seated at her desk, an old steel one left behind when the school closed, Paige frowned at Lori, who stood in the doorframe. She nodded toward one of the two chairs in front of the desk. When Lori sat down, her boss dipped a hand into a one-hundred-calorie pack of Chips Ahoy and said, "You're a little hot right now."

"Come on," Lori said. "Nobody reads that damn paper anyway."

"Everyone reads that darn paper, sweetie." Paige tipped the cookie bag toward Lori, hoping this gesture of kindness would keep things calm and cool. "And everyone listens to the Bear."

"I was only joking." Lori took one tiny cookie. "They know that, right?"

Paige stared at her employee and wondered how she might explain this. The naiveté of some people never ceased to amaze. Of course everyone knew it was a joke. They didn't care. That was the plainest thing nowadays. People only want to gripe about how awful and stupid and inappropriate everyone else is. They don't want to do anything or learn anything or even care about anything. They just want to bemoan this or that, to lay blame, to decry, to get outraged. And here was Lori with her master's from the Hubert H. Humphrey Institute, for God's sake, and still she was clueless. Sometimes Paige wanted to shake her, snap her into reality, get her to grow up. But Lori was a gentle and tiny thing. She had the build of a woman who had been a gymnast or a diver in high school, thin and strong with a little cherub's face. But she looked sharp in a pantsuit, and her small, bookish eyeglasses lent her an air of intellectualism without making her come off like a bitch.

These things were important factors when Paige hired Lori, though she'd never admit to that. Lori was around thirty-five but looked twenty-five, while Paige was fifty-five and looked every day of it. It wasn't hard to figure that local officials, regardless of gender, didn't much enjoy the affordable-housing harangue from a middle-aged woman with weight-management issues, but they were all ears for a pretty young thing pitching community enhancement through economically diverse neighborhood development.

After eating the last of the cookies, Paige said, "Distraction is the safest thing in government—in all life, I suppose. If you don't like an idea, you complain about the people who do. You question their motives or their worthiness. Then you never have to defend yourself. You never have to have an idea of your own."

"I have no idea what you're talking about," Lori said.

Both women laughed, though for different reasons.

"Those people know me," Lori said. "I'll just go in there all business-as-usual, and it'll be fine."

"Was that a joke or were you serious?" Paige stopped laughing and turned stern-faced. "I really couldn't tell."

Duane Ubel knew two things for certain: Petco was worse than the Mafia, and this idiot letter to the editor was the last thing he needed. He was up to his eyeballs just to get doors open over at the Spaw, and if it didn't take off, he might as well start looking for a trailer park to die in. That's how bad it was, and it was all the fault of Petco.

He opened the phone book on his kitchen counter and looked up the woman who'd written the letter. Of course, the husband answered—friendly as could be—and said the wife was still at work, and he wondered who was calling and if he could take a message.

"Here's the message," Duane said. "Please tell that wife of yours that I never asked for any of this. I ran the pet store over by the old mall for twenty years, and I never wanted to do anything else. Understood?"

"What?" Kent said. "Who is this?"

"This is Duane Ubel. *Who is this?* Who do you think?" Duane's wife had gone to dinner with a friend, so he was free to raise his voice and speak bluntly. "Cross out that crap I said before. I've got a new message for your wife. You tell her that if someone wants to crash a plane into any-fucking-thing, they ought to do it at the fucking Petco headquarters."

"Okay, maybe I should hang up now." Safe on the other end of the line, Kent wore a broad smile. The fact was that he hadn't heard anything so funny in a long time, although he knew he should be upset, offended, possibly even outraged. "I'll give Lori the message."

Duane heard a chuckle, which was more than he could bear. "Listen, you smartass," he said. "You know what Petco does when they come into your town? They hire away your fucking groomer, for one thing. Then they undercut you on the fucking Iams and every other goddamn thing. Then they strong-arm the fucking vet into working for them because if he doesn't, they'll just run him out of business. Which is what they do to you."

"Okay," said Kent, interested now but still grinning wildly. "Then what?"

"Then what? You close." Duane had stopped shouting. "You close the store you've had since your kids were just babies, and you try real hard to think of some way to make a living so you can keep your house and keep your kids in college and keep some food on the table. Then you go begging at the bank."

"Lori didn't mean anything," he said. "It was just a joke. It wasn't even her joke. It was mine, really. I said it to her, and she . . . well, you know what she did."

"You need lots of money because one day you get an idea." Duane wanted to finish his story and hadn't quite heard what Kent said. "You realize that the only thing you can do is go further. You sell things Petco could never sell, things like space and security and caring and whatever other bullshit you can think of. And you have to go all in. You have to make it beautiful or nobody will want to pay for it."

"Makes sense," said Kent, sitting on an arm of the sofa and staring through the front window at black and gray roofs of houses and downtown buildings, orange and gold leaves on the trees of the river valley's opposite slope, and wide-open blue skies above. He didn't feel like arguing. "That all makes perfect sense."

"You think so?" Duane's voice turned quieter. He took some long breaths and sniffed once—loudly, the way older men do. "You'll have to pardon me. I've always had a temper."

"It's okay."

"Not really." Duane sighed. "These things have been difficult. That's all. Very difficult. And then I find myself made out to be a terrorist."

"No, no," Kent said. "That's not it. That's the opposite. The joke was that your business is just the kind of thing terrorists must hate about us."

There was silence on the line until Duane cleared this throat. "Is that," he spoke slowly, "supposed to make me feel better?"

"No, I guess not." Now Kent wished he'd have just hung up when Duane was lobbing the F-bombs, rather than bothering with explanations. "The joke was just a comment, I guess, about how so many people have nothing and we have so much

Not Funny

that we can treat dogs so well. That's all. It just popped into my head, and I said it."

"I wish it had ended there."

Trying to sound chipper, Kent said, "Maybe you're onto something. Maybe you should write a letter saying all the stuff you just told me, saying someone ought to crash a plane into Petco."

Duane Ubel sighed again and said, "That's not funny."

Lori remembered where she was when the men crashed the planes into the buildings. Of course she did. Everyone did. And the where-were-you talks were the most boring thing in the world. What she thought about now, these strange years later, was not where she had been but what it had meant, what had crystallized when she stared out the window of her office that morning. From a space four stories from the top of the second-tallest building in downtown St. Paul, the second-largest city in a state half a country removed from those men and their airplanes, she saw a cloudless blue sky stretching over the black water of the river, the glaring white concrete of failed industry on the west-side flats, the just-turning trees on the distant bluff. What a lovely morning it was.

Standing at that window, Lori made some calculations. If people were doing this on purpose, if that could really be, how many planes would they need before they'd bother with this place? How far down the list were she and the other workers in St. Paul's old First Bank Building? She comprehended how far removed she really was, how little her place mattered outside of its borders, what a luxury that could be.

In the other room, a half-dozen co-workers still gathered around their boss' thirteen-inch television, watching smoke rise and discussing whether the fires could be extinguished or whether they'd just have to burn themselves out. Lori knew there weren't enough planes or enough hijackers. No jetliner would streak down toward this city, level its glinting wings over the empty flats, and take aim at a building anonymous to the distant world.

Her husband phoned and asked, "Are you afraid?"

"Not at all," she said.

"How'd you like to be some poor SOB in an office? You're sitting at your desk. You look out the window. There it is." Back then Kent was teaching at a high school out in the suburbs. The kids had been allowed to watch the news coverage on classroom televisions. "Can you imagine?"

"What if you didn't have a window?" Lori asked. She imagined a young woman who looked like her, only better dressed and prettier. The woman occupied a cubicle deep in an office interior, a cube among a hundred cubes. "What a thing to die for, just some job."

Except in deepest winter, Ryan LeVander never wore socks to work. He might put on some khakis, maybe pick out an ironed shirt, but on his feet he wore only some old Stan Smiths or beat-up brown loafers. His editor—a tight-ass with half his experience—had given up complaining about it, but Ryan could see her gaze drop when he walked in, could spot the tiny frown or the quick shake of her head.

"What's your column this week?" she asked when he arrived that day. She had been talking to the chick who covered cops and courts, and she just stood there, hands on hips, in the middle of the newsroom. "If it's late this week, we'll slap something else in the hole."

"Oh, it's gold," he said. "No worries this time."

"Don't pull some dumb story off the wire and make a bunch of wisecracks about it." The editor didn't bother to lower her voice. "Even our readers can see that for what it is, LeVander."

"Oh, yeah?" Ryan sat down, rocked back in his chair, and crossed his legs. He smiled at the cops and courts girl, and glanced around at the handful of others in the room, all pretending not to hear. "And what is it?"

"A lot of ego and not a lot of effort," the editor said.

The cops and courts chick snorted.

Sometimes Ryan wanted to choke the both of them. They were know-it-all shits. But he understood something they seemed not to. The joke was on them. They had chosen a doomed business, and all the upward mobility in the universe wasn't enough to pull them out of that black hole.

Whistling as he dialed, Ryan placed a call over to The Spaw. One interview, he figured, and an hour or so to bang out the column—another for his weekly slot, a little bone the boss had tossed him when she pulled him out of sports and made him do the G.A. thing, like some kid straight from college.

A woman answered at The Spaw, and Ryan asked for the owner. Duane came onto the line and, with hardly any convincing, started spewing about the letter to the editor and the bitch who wrote it.

"You try to do something good, to contribute something to this community, and then something like this happens," the owner said. "It's the pits, really the pits."

This Duane guy was a real talker. Ryan just threw in an *uh-huh* or an *okay* now and then, and steered things back on track after Duane started on some tangent about Petco and big-box retailers and the impossible position of the small-business man.

"How did you feel when you read that letter?" Ryan asked.

"Sick, just sick," Duane said. "I didn't understand why someone would say such a thing. My own damn son's a veteran, for Christ's sake."

"Uh-huh," Ryan said.

"Pardon my French," Duane said. "I get upset when I talk about this. It's very hurtful. You can understand."

"Uh-huh."

Ryan scratched out notes as Duane went on and on. This would be a breeze, an utter breeze. Set it up with an anecdote about a hardworking man who sits down for breakfast, opens his morning paper, and finds his business made out to be something awful and crass, maybe even something evil. Yes, evil. He'd definitely have to get that word in early. After the set-up, he'd give a graph or two of background, quote the letter, and string together a few more of Duane's quotes. He'd have to play up that nugget about the son being a veteran. Too good, too good.

As they wrapped up the interview, something surprising happened. Ryan thought of the perfect question.

"What if you lived in the Third World, Iraq or someplace, and you heard about The Spaw?" he asked. "What would you think if you heard American dogs get pedicures and soak in Jacuzzi tubs?

"Jesus," Duane said. "I thought you were understanding me."

"I'm only playing devil's advocate."

"Well, let me think," Duane said. After a long pause, he took a big breath and spoke. "I'd think what a great country that must be. That's what I'd think. I'd wish my country could be more like that."

Every softball team has a fat guy, and on Kent's team it was Bo Zielski—the king of the pop-out and the loudest mouth on the field. Kent didn't like Bo, and as far as he could tell, neither did anyone else on the squad. Yet there he was, the man with the iron glove. Bo yelled at the ump, ridiculed opponents, and embarrassed his wife, but when a teammate once asked him to tone it down, he said, "Fuck that, man. This is my outlet."

The team had been swept in a doubleheader and had gone to T.J. Finnegan's, a downtown bar where Bud went for five bucks a pitcher and where on weeknights, even during fall ball, nearly every grown man in the place would have a number on his back. Bo wore number sixty-nine. This also embarrassed his wife.

Not Funny

"Was that your chick that LeVander ripped the other day?" Bo asked. The team members had pushed together a few tables at the back of the bar, and by pure misfortune, Kent wound up across from Bo.

"I didn't see the paper," Kent said.

"Yeah, right," Bo replied. "What'd she do? Didn't she say the 9/11 bombers ought to blast the fuckin' pet shop?"

"There were no bombs on September eleventh." Kent had his eyes on the TV screen over Bo's head, and he pretended to be intensely interested in what it showed, which happened to be an advertisement for an erectile dysfunction medication.

"Whatever." Bo glanced at the TV, but turned back. "Is she one of those PETA freaks or what's her deal?"

"Why would PETA want to crash a plane into a kennel?"

The other guys around them all leaned back from the table and took it in. This was something they could laugh about once Bo got piss-drunk and wandered off to bother an old classmate from high school or some other poor soul he happened to know.

"Whatever." Bo nodded at his teammates. "She must be some kinda liberal whacko or femi-Nazi or whatever."

Kent frowned. Bo could piss you off, but it wasn't worth arguing with him. You might as well debate world politics with a lamppost. Waving a hand dismissively, Kent said, "It was a joke. It was a satirical comment meant to call attention to the grotesque consumption made possible by widespread affluence among Americans and their shamelessness and sense of entitlement."

"What the fuck?" Bo went slack-jawed and shook his head as if waking from a stupor, then looked around to see if he got any laughs. He didn't. Still, he pushed on, "I got a joke for you. Get this: Do you know what PETA stands for?"

"Damn, Bo," one of the guys said. "That joke is ancient."

"And it was shit in the first place," another one added.

Kent smirked.

It Takes You Over

"It means People Eating Tasty Animals." Bo chuckled at his punch line. "That's what PETA means."

Someone picked up the pitcher and refilled Bo's beer for him.

"Come on, you assholes. Don't you understand? That's satire of . . ." He sipped from the glass. "It's all about America's conspicuous consumption of various animals and whatnot."

Kent couldn't help but laugh. For Bo, that was not bad—borderline clever, even if unintentionally so. Some of the other guys laughed, too. Bo smiled a satisfied smile, and tipped his glass at Kent as if toasting him.

"Tell your wife that one," Bo said. "And you ought to tell her to knock off the letters to the paper."

"I will," Kent said.

"Joke or no, it was pretty stupid." Bo watched something over Kent's head as he said this. "There's nothing funny about terrorists."

Hearing a half-drunk loudmouth talk about Lori this way made Kent squeamish, and he felt he should set the record straight. He should explain to Bo—to all of the guys—that the joke had really been his, not his wife's. He should admit that it wasn't born of qualms about American excess, but had come to mind without any supporting rationale. It wasn't a window to his soul, but now he wished it had been. He wished he could be a more thoughtful, passionate person. He wished he'd cared enough to write a letter.

All he said was "Screw it, Bo. Can't a joke just be a joke?"

The high school's memorial poetry slam had taken place on September 11, 2002, and for the most part, it was every bit as painful as Lori expected. The kids sure tried. She had to credit them for that. It couldn't have been easy to get up in front of an auditorium full of uncomfortable parents and judgmental classmates. Still, the listening hurt.

One girl offered this simile: "The bodies fell like teardrops."

Another went this route: "Black smoke rose from the heroes' pyre / their souls, our innocence drifting higher and higher."

When Lori buried her face in her hands, Kent elbowed her and gave her a look. His experience with his students made him immune to the cringe-worthy moments. He could bear it all with a smile. He could find something constructive to say after even the most misguided oral presentation on, say, the temperance movement or the sexual revolution.

One greasy-haired boy began relatively promisingly: "Consider the box cutter / Consider the men and their box cutters / Consider the box cutter against flesh."

This specific image of violence had penetrated the evening's politeness and sentimentality. The audience had had to consider the hand of one man, the mundane tool it held, the damage it inflicted. The air went out of the room. But the boy's grip on his audience was momentary, for his poem would then take focus on his job at the supermarket, where he would swing his box cutter and slash open boxes of goods, where he would accidentally gash his left thumb, where as he sucked blood from the wound he would, strangely, be reminded of those other men, the nineteen and the box cutters they carried. He paused before his closing line, then spoke haltingly: "Even the box cutter, the lowly blade, can destroy the world."

Lori suppressed a groan. The problem, she concluded, was the kids couldn't get outside of their own experience. Not in any real way. Not in any way that wasn't corny or predictable. Physical distance and the filter of television bound the kids' understanding of the world. These things stunted their sense of empathy, prevented them from thinking beyond teardrops and smoke.

But the kids weren't alone. When she had stood at her office window that day and stared out from the second-tallest building in St. Paul, she felt no connection to the things she'd seen on television. She knew no one in New York or

Washington. Her closest personal tie had been through a former employer, a supervisor at her first job out of college. The woman had grown up in the Bronx, and the running joke in the office was that within fifteen minutes of meeting someone, the woman would mention her New York roots. Never failed. "I grew up in the Bronx so I like to be direct," she'd say, or, "I grew up in the Bronx so don't worry about hurting my feelings."

At lunchtime, Lori and her colleagues would laugh. "She grew up in the Bronx, so what?" they'd say. "She's got that in common with about ten million other idiots."

As the young poets droned on, Lori thought back to that day, thought how at first she hadn't hurt for those people, how the scenes on TV were only spectacle. She thought how that changed only when she imagined the office worker—the better-looking, better-dressed version of herself—sitting unhappily in a cubicle, dying for a job she didn't like, never seeing it coming. So it seemed, Lori realized with dread, she herself wasn't much more sophisticated or sensitive than the kids.

The memorial poetry slam's last reader had been a blockheaded boy with a pup-stache and hairline already in retreat. As he began reading in a quiet baritone, the sound of shuffling in the audience—people preparing to go home—mostly drowned out the opening lines. But the crowd quieted, and the boy went ahead. He never mentioned planes or buildings or falling bodies or fiery pits or teardrops or smoke. He merely listed all the television shows he had missed because of news coverage from New York, Washington, Pennsylvania, Boston, Montreal, Chicago, Los Angeles, and distant sites of militant training camps. He called out the names of dozens of shows, and finally he closed by saying, "What about my *Friends*? / How long would I wait? / Forty-eight hours/ Forty-eight hours until six sexy singles popped open their umbrellas / Forty-eight hours was all it would take."

A few beats of silence passed before someone chuckled. Then a few others laughed. Kent laughed. Lori laughed. Most everyone laughed. Applause rose from the audience. The blockheaded boy smiled.

"That's pretty good," Kent said. "That's funny."

Paige sat behind Lori's desk and waited for her to arrive. On the drive in that morning, she'd listened to the Bear, and the talk had once again been about The Spaw, Lori's letter to the editor, liberal self-loathing, disrespecting the troops. This had been going on more than a week. The time had come to act, Paige decided. She'd been waiting at Lori's desk for half an hour and was well into her third Nutri-Grain bar.

"Hey, Paige," Lori said when she came in, with dark dots on the shoulders of her yellow blouse and her hair damp from the rain. "What's up?"

"Did you listen to the radio?" Paige replied.

"Oh, no. Not again. What'd they say this time?"

"Sit," Paige said, nodding toward the chair normally reserved for visitors. "We're going to put an end to this."

"How?"

Paige squared herself behind the computer and wiggled the mouse. "We're writing your apology."

"I can't apologize." Lori sat down with her purse in her lap. "It won't do any good."

"Wrong-o, Lori. An apology settles everything. We'll give it the old *I'm truly sorry if my words caused pain to anyone.*"

Lori laughed. "I love that one. *I'm not sorry I said it. I'm just sorry people didn't like it.* Clever."

Paige navigated to *The Daily Eagle* website and clicked to the opinion page, then clicked again on *Send a letter to the editor*. She typed "Apology to The Spaw" in the subject line and moved the cursor to the empty text box.

"Let's go. You talk and I'll type."

"What should I say? My husband's joke was tasteless and horrible, and I'm sorry I ripped it off and sent it to the paper? Would that work?"

"Your husband?" Paige cocked her head and waited for clarification.

"It was his joke." Lori slumped into the chair. "I read him the story while he was making breakfast, and he said the thing about the airplane. I thought it was funny, so I clicked a couple buttons, framed it with the crap about why people loathe Americans, and sent it off."

"Why not put his name on it?"

"He wouldn't let me."

Paige shook her head and mumbled, "Jeez."

"What?"

"Nothing. Let's get back to the apology."

"I can't apologize." Lori sat up and tossed her bag onto the desk. "I appreciate it, but can't we just get to work?"

"Nonsense." Paige scowled. "You can apologize, and you don't even have to mean it."

"An apology affirms everything they've said about me."

"It doesn't," Paige said.

"That's the world." Lori's voice sounded suddenly confident, righteous even. "To apologize is to capitulate. If I apologize, then they've been right all along and everything they've said goes unchallenged."

"Who?"

"The dog spa asshole and the idiots on the radio."

"That's the power of the non-apology. You say you're sorry about their response, not about what you did."

"It doesn't matter," Lori said. "The mere utterance of the word 'sorry' is an admission of defeat."

"*Utterance*, ugh," Paige put her head down on the desk. "Why does everyone have to be impossible?"

Not Funny

Barry Swanum went off the air at 9 o'clock, but he never stopped being the Bear. In a city of this size, people knew you, especially when you'd been around as long as Barry. The waitresses at Applebee's knew him. So did the staffers at the YMCA's front desk. So did the girls at the DQ. So did the starter at the public golf course. These were the places where he spent his open afternoons.

"Hey, Bear, let me give you a tip," said Lon Bergstad, the retired P.E. teacher who worked at Prairie View for a small wage and all the free golf he could handle.

"What is it?" Barry said. He was headed out for nine holes. Golfing alone was one of life's little-known pleasures. Late in the season, there would be no threesome of college kids to stick him with. Lon would send him out onto the mostly empty course by himself. "Are the greens slow?"

Lon was a compact, solid man. He looked like he might have been a wrestler in his day, way back in the 1950s or '60s, and he always wore crisp slacks, a nice golf shirt, and, on days like this one, a matching windbreaker. Barry felt like a fat slob beside him, and he assumed Lon thought there was something less than serious about a career in radio.

"Not that kind of tip." Lon waved Barry off when he raised his receipt to prove he'd paid up. "I heard you talking about Duane."

"Who?"

"Duane Ubel."

"Who?"

"Owns the daycare for dogs?"

"Oh, yeah," Barry said. "The dog guy."

"Right. The one dodging all the airplanes."

Barry laughed.

Lon smirked, stepped close to Barry, and spoke conspiratorially. "I coached his boy, and I'm afraid his dad is misleading people."

"That so?"

"This business about his son being a veteran?" Lon raised his eyebrows. "He wasn't exactly hunting down Saddam. He was in the National Guard. Did a spell of security detail in Kosovo. Back home safe and sound without ever raising his gun."

"Well, he did his bit, right?" Barry didn't much care about Duane or his son. He wanted to tee off and get out there. "Doesn't really matter where he served, does it?"

Lon frowned and stepped away. He gave Barry a hard look and said, "Just thought you might like to know the truth."

"Fair enough," Barry said. "That thing has about run its course regardless. Don't let it bother you."

"Can't help but get bothered sometimes." Lon spoke over his shoulder as he walked away. "World's full of whiners. Everyone's a victim these days. Everyone's been wronged."

Even you, Barry thought as he strode up to the tee box. He thought it but didn't say it. That was another thing he understood about radio, about life in general: What you don't say is just as important as what you do.

He pulled out the driver, took a few practice swings, and let it rip. He knew immediately that he'd gotten every bit of it but that he'd left the face open again. The ball soared high, curled right, and kept tracking right, right, right over into the next fairway. The sky was big and blue and beautiful, though, and Barry didn't mind the walk.

Kent craned his neck through the gap between the shower curtain and the wall. Lori had her back turned, one arm held high as she scratched at her armpit with a pink plastic razor. Water hissed from the showerhead, drummed against her skin, sloshed at her feet.

"Hey," he said.

Her body seized, and she made a little yelp.

"Sorry." Kent stepped back and pulled the shower curtain partially open. "You gotta get out here."

"What do you want?"

"Come hear the Bear."

"Oh, no." Lori turned, let her shoulders droop, and stared at Kent with tired eyes. "Not again."

"Not you." Kent gestured for her to get moving. "Come on."

"Why?"

"Let's go!" he half-shouted.

"I've only got one pit shaved!" she half-shouted back.

"Lori, you need to hear this." Kent cranked the lever to shut off the water. "Some illegal immigrant crashed his pickup into one of those casino buses."

"No!"

"It's true." He handed his wife a towel. "He blew through a stop sign out on eighty-three. Guy had no papers, speaks no English. They don't even know his real name."

"Did anyone die?"

"No. Just broken bones, cuts, contusions, whatever." Kent smiled, and Lori smiled back, a wide goofball smile. He loved seeing her like this—uncovered, the pale skin on her shoulders, the lean muscle of her small body, her eyes suddenly energetic and happy again. She hurried through drying off and told him to pass her the robe hanging on the door.

"This is exactly what you needed," Kent said. "It's a godsend."

They sat at the kitchen table and listened to the Bear. Kent poured coffee, but no one made breakfast. The driver, apparently a Mexican who had come north to do farm work, was locked in the county jail, where he'd given police no fewer than three names and then quit talking altogether. The callers were incensed. What had become of this state? Couldn't a busload of seniors go off to Treasure Island without some illegal broadsiding them? Conditioner drying in her hair, Lori sat with Kent and listened until he had to rush off to make his first-hour class.

As he zipped his coat, he said, "What a shitstorm this will be."

"I hope you're right." Lori stood beside him in the foyer, her hands deep in the pockets of her robe. "I want to get back to normal life."

"You're in the clear." He bent and kissed her forehead. "The illegal immigrant's got you beat, hands down."

Lori stood inside the storm door and watched as Kent backed his car from the driveway, shifted gears, and accelerated away down the street. He hadn't looked her way, hadn't waved goodbye, but she didn't mind. Morning was coming on cold and clear, and the sun was rising into a perfectly blue, perfectly empty sky over the low buildings of their distracted city.

Lives
of Great
Northerners

With pain and pressure gathering in her abdomen, Marilyn ran the back of her wrist across her forehead, gazed toward the floor, and wondered if the IRS man would ever leave. He stood in the foyer—tie loosened, jacket unbuttoned—and looked around. He was about Marilyn's age, and he wore the broad necktie and wide lapels that had become fashionable.

"Is that a new furniture set, Mrs. Boyne?" he asked. "I'm certain my wife would admire it."

She shook her head. Her insides tightened as if gripped in a fist. Sweat moistened her neck, her hairline, the small of her back. The fist released.

"Sure is a lovely home you've got—full of lovely things," the man said, his shoulders going slack as he scanned the room, as if he'd entered a grand church or civic building and not a three-bedroom ranch house just like the others along this block, the next block, the next. "Remind me, Mrs. Boyne, how does your husband make his living?"

With her nine-year-old, Rosemary, now standing close behind her and tugging on the tail of her blouse, Marilyn tilted her head and glanced dull-eyed at the IRS man. She had told him before that Dave was a plumber, and she knew that he was asking again only to see her reaction, to gauge her fear. She had good reason to be afraid, having hidden those papers in her bedroom, but she had to trust that this man would never imagine her capable of such an act, would never bother to ask what she knew of her father's business affairs. But what if he did ask?

A chill rattled her shoulders; then the fist squeezed her insides again, more forcefully than before. Something about his face troubled her. His eyes were too close together, his lips slightly too large, locked in a false grin. The man had the look of a television preacher—or the type of fellow you wouldn't leave alone with your children.

From Marilyn's belly came a strange noise—a gurgle like the last of the water running down the bathtub drain, loud enough for all to hear.

She winced, and the man shook his head. He looked at Rosemary in the pitying way that people so often did, which ordinarily annoyed Marilyn but which she now hoped was a sign of genuine sympathy for her family's problems.

Rosemary stepped back and smiled. "Oh, boy," she said in her deep, slow-tongued voice. "Your tummy's hungry."

"I'd better be on my way," the man said. He patted the briefcase into which he, after two hours of searching, had placed several documents from the cabinets stored in Marilyn's basement, along with dozens of canceled checks he'd sifted from the decades' worth piled in the old steamer chest. "Now you're certain that those are all of your father's records? I couldn't find a return for seventy-two."

"He's got the recent ones," Marilyn said.

"That's right. I'd forgotten," the man replied. "Sure there isn't anything else around?"

"That's it," Marilyn said, her voice barely above a whisper. She placed her hand over her stomach, covering the spot below the waistline of her slacks where the pressure felt most severe.

"Because, you know," he continued, "any information we gather now will only help conclude matters more quickly, Mrs. Boyne, so everyone can get on with life."

The IRS agent leaned in, smiled conspiringly, and said, "I don't care what sort of racket your father was running. I just want to clear up his income reporting, see that the government gets what it's owed."

Marilyn nodded, and when the man walked out, she broke for the bathroom.

Of all the things Larry Ingerson learned during ten years of formal schooling, none stuck with him more than the story of James J. Hill. Larry was in ninth grade when Hill passed away, and soon after the death in 1916, Larry's history teacher distributed copies of a commemorative booklet printed by one of the St. Paul newspapers. It bore the title "The Life of a Great Northerner," and it explained how Hill, born in Ontario in 1838, had arrived at the St. Paul levee as a young man with little more than the clothes on his back and a few dollars in his pocket.

Beginning his career as a shipping clerk, Hill got his education not at some fancy college but through twenty years of work for companies that transported goods along the rivers of the Upper Midwest. In 1878, he and other investors purchased the failing St. Paul and Pacific Railroad, which Hill then built into the mighty Great Northern Railroad. He pushed his line north into Canada and west through the Rockies and to the Pacific, all the while accumulating a vast fortune that allowed him to build for himself the largest home inside Minnesota's borders. He once said, "When we are all dead and gone, the sun will still shine, the rain will fall, and this railroad will run as usual."

Larry loved that line, never doubted it. He read through the booklet again and again, wishing he could one day be Hill's sort of man, wondering if he had the mettle, trying to convince himself he did.

While Rosemary perched on the edge of the tub, Marilyn endured an explosive round of diarrhea. The noises—outlandish and impatient—rose and subsided, then returned and subsided again. Marilyn felt some small relief, knowing this particular sort of suffering was specific and short-lived. She would not go to bed tonight worrying about it. She would not have to explain it to her father and her husband. She would not have to answer a litany of questions about it.

"Done yet, Mom?" Rosemary asked.

"Almost," Marilyn replied.

Rosemary stared at her, directly at her midsection, which was bare and bent atop the toilet.

"Rosie, please," Marilyn said.

Rosemary jerked her head away—orange hair swirling into her face—and looked out through the bathroom's open doorway. Marilyn would have preferred to endure her bout of abdominal distress alone, but an averted gaze was what passed for privacy when she and her daughter were alone together, as they were most days since the other kids had returned to school.

Marilyn was happy to have her youngest at home. She welcomed the company, and she could not live with the idea of sending her to the public school, where retarded children were segregated, even eating lunch after the other kids had gone to the playground.

When her stomach calmed, she led her daughter back downstairs and inspected what the IRS man had left behind. He was tidy about his work, and Marilyn understood enough to know that the man hadn't really known what he was looking for. His previous visits had yielded nothing, and he'd come back to fish around for something, anything.

Inside the steamer chest sat piles of shoeboxes, each filled with canceled checks and marked by year on the lid. The checks stopped three years earlier—around the time her parents had sold their house, moved into a seniors' high-rise downtown, and brought their papers and dusty knickknacks to be stored at Marilyn and Dave's. She had seen the IRS man remove checks dating from 1968 to 1971, the year her father retired.

The chest also held mementoes of her father's career with the railroad. Rosemary had found a cigarette lighter—a heavy stainless steel thing that bore the Great Northern logo, a mountain goat perched on a rocky peak and peering, as Marilyn saw it, ever westward. The girl now flipped the lid open and clicked it closed, repeating this action again and again.

"Be careful with that," Marilyn said, though she knew the wick was gone, the flint shot, and the chamber dry. "My dad kept that on his desk. He used to let me try it when I was your age."

"It's Dad's?" Rosemary held up the lighter and considered it.

"My dad, honey," Marilyn said. "Your grandpa—Grandpa Larry."

Rosemary flipped the top back and forth—click-clack, click-clack, click-clack—until it broke loose, skipped across the concrete floor, and disappeared into the shadows under the washtub.

Larry Ingerson grew up in Stillwater, Minnesota, a river town thirty miles east of St. Paul. His father was a grocer and a gambler, his mother a teetotaler and stalwart at her Lutheran church. They had two children—both boys, Larry being the first. Soon after Larry turned sixteen, his father lost his store due to gambling debts—and then the family home.

Larry soon announced plans to quit school and get full-time work, leaving home over his mother's tearful objections and his father's threat to knock sense into him. With a worn copy of "The Life of a Great Northerner" in his suitcase, Larry headed for St. Paul, where he found a bed in an Eastside boarding house and pleaded his way into a job on the docks at the Great Northern warehouse.

In those early days, he thought often of the young James J. Hill and considered himself fortunate to be a cog in the mighty machine Hill built. Larry would ascend through the corporate ranks slowly and only by dint of his determination. By the mid-forties, he would be the senior man in the purchasing department, and finally in 1959, he would be made vice president of purchasing and inventory.

Channel 5 replayed Woody Woodpecker cartoons at 2:30 and Casper at 3 o'clock—a daily blessing, as far as Marilyn was concerned. Rosemary sat on the floor, very near the television. Normally Marilyn would have ordered her to move back, but today she couldn't muster the energy to care. She lay motionless on the couch, drapes drawn over the picture window behind her.

Jan arrived home from school first. She was a sophomore that fall, while the boys still had two more years over at the junior high. Timothy and Patrick were twins, and at home they were considered a single unit. Two halves of a whole. *The boys.* "God, Mom," Jan said, swinging in through the front door and dropping her book bag—a transparent plastic one printed with large daisies—on the nearest armchair. She shrugged out of her yellow windbreaker, balled it up, and crammed it into the open mouth of the bag. "It stinks in here."

"Is that any way to say hello?" Marilyn asked. Rosemary shushed them, then groaned as Jan pulled the drapery cord to let in some daylight, which glared onto the television screen. Cross-legged on the carpet, Rosemary shuffled nearer the console. Marilyn looked at the screen in the same dull-eyed way she'd stared down the IRS man.

"What's wrong with you?" Jan asked. "Are you sick again?"

"The IRS came back."

After Rosemary reached and cranked up the volume, Jan perched herself sideways on the edge of the sofa. She wore a loose white shirt, collarless and wide-necked, and some snug corduroys she had picked out when her father took her back-to-school shopping at the new mall. Marilyn thought she was becoming a pretty young woman, a dangerous thing.

"Why?" Jan asked. "What did Grandpa do? I wish somebody would tell the truth around here."

Marilyn looked her oldest child in the eyes, considered for a moment, and nodded. "Here it is, as I see it." She pushed herself onto one elbow, moving closer to Jan so they could converse despite the blaring television.

Jan sat up and pulled in her chin, her expression at once surprised and suspicious.

"Your grandfather was part of the old guard at the railroad, and once they got in trouble, the new guard went looking for someone to blame."

"What does that mean?" Jan shrugged and opened her palms. "That doesn't help."

Marilyn sighed. She had hoped a little information would be enough. The answers she'd received from her father were much like the answer she'd just given—broad, largely meaningless. Any important information Marilyn gathered—and she had quite a bit of it—had been acquired on her own.

"Well, honey, people don't do business the way they used to," she said. "Your grandfather was in charge of purchasing for the entire railroad. Other than payroll, any money going out had to go through him. People used to want to be his friend, to win his favor, to help him out."

Jan stiffened and whispered, "They think he took kickbacks?"

Kickbacks. The word surprised Marilyn. She hadn't expected it, especially from a teenager, but she appreciated its directness.

"Yes," she said. "That's what they think."

It Takes You Over

The railroad dominated Larry's life, occupying his thoughts and consuming his time and energy as he grew from a round-faced teenager into a lean but powerful man in his mid-twenties. He wore his light hair slicked back off his forehead and always looked neat, even when exerting himself on the loading dock. At twenty-five, Larry decided it was time to marry—even Hill, after all, had made time for a wife and children—and three years later he found a willing girl from the Eastside.

Larry and Gladys had two children, first a girl named Marilyn, then a boy. They named the boy Charles after Larry's younger brother, even though Larry always thought his brother was something of a dandy. Larry always called his son by his full name. Never Charlie. Certainly not Chuck.

In the early 1940s, Larry moved his family to an affluent neighborhood on the western side of St. Paul, just blocks from the river, which was tree-lined and quiet that far upstream from the city's noisy levee and filthy railyards. By the time Charles was old enough to spend a morning at work with his father, Larry had moved to a large office far from the loading docks.

Marilyn opened the tap, let the water run hot into the tub, and shook in some Dreft powder, which her husband called "the poor-man's bubble-bath." The bathroom was situated at the end of the hallway, between the master bedroom and the room the boys shared. Leaving the door cracked, she undressed and settled into the steaming water. If she leaned far enough over the edge of the tub, she could see Jan's outstretched legs. Her older girl had joined the younger one on the living room carpet, where, if allowed, they would gladly pass the entire evening watching the TV, which their father referred to as "the idiot box."

The hot bath relaxed Marilyn—easing tension in her jaw muscles, which she'd unknowingly clenched all afternoon, and comforted her digestive system. She liked the babyish smell of the laundry soap, liked the way it made her skin feel soft and slick. She ran her palms up and down over her thighs, stomach, and chest, and she eased down into the water so only her knees and head protruded above the bubbles.

She replayed in her mind the telephone conversation she'd just had with her father. She had called him after earlier visits from the IRS man, and he had sounded relaxed, even dismissive. He usually apologized for storing his papers in her house and explained how there just wasn't room in their unit and how the storage area in the building's basement didn't seem secure. But this time, he hadn't said anything like that.

"What did the agent say?" he asked. "Did he ask about your brother?"

"What's Charles got to do with this?" Marilyn knew the answer to her question, but she couldn't let her father find out that she'd been through the papers, that she'd seen the letters that had him worried. She also figured that if Charles' name had come up, her father had reason to worry the IRS might be on the trail of some misdirected money.

"Charles ought to have nothing to do with it," he said. "These men are on a goose chase, a witch hunt, whatever you call it."

"I know, Dad," she said.

Her father went quiet on the other end of the line. For a moment, Marilyn thought this was the time to finally set him straight—to stop pussyfooting around and explain what she had done. She wished she could muster the courage to do it, but she was afraid he would be angry or ashamed—or both. She said nothing.

"What *did* he ask about?" he asked.

She could imagine him there—in the kitchen of the apartment, whispering so her mother wouldn't hear. His face had

It Takes You Over

grown jowly with the years but remained ever cheery, or seemingly so. He still wore a shirt and tie most days, as he had done throughout most of his working life, even when he was a young foreman on the docks.

"Oh, Dad," she said. "The same as before—except he wondered how Dave and I could afford new furniture."

"You got new furniture?"

"No," she said. "That's what I'm saying. With him, it's all funny business. Everything's suspicious."

The conversation had ended there, and as she reconsidered it in the bathtub, she cupped water into her hands and splashed her face. She put her fingertips on her forehead, rubbing slowly above her closed eyes, trying to clear her head, to think of something else, something pleasant.

Just then, the sound of hurried, heavy footsteps boomed from the hallway. Rosemary dashed into the room with her jeans already unsnapped and her hand on the zipper.

"Gotta wee! Gotta wee!" she said, jogging in place as she opened her fly and wiggled her underwear down. "Gotta wee bad!"

The sounds of Rosemary plopping onto the toilet seat and her burst of urine splashing in the bowl came almost simultaneously. Marilyn couldn't help but laugh.

After she'd wiped and flushed, Rosemary kicked off her jeans and underwear. She pulled her T-shirt over her head and got one foot into the water before her mother could do anything to stop her.

"Rosie, no!" Marilyn said, but it was no use. Suds splashed and the water rose nearly to the lip of the tub as the girl wedged her frame into the gap between Marilyn's knees.

Rosemary put her face under the water—her whole head, nearly—and blew a motorboat, as was her custom. Coming up for air, she held her eyes closed and sprayed suds and water away from her mouth. The look on her face was one of joy, though she complained, "Too hot!"

Marilyn went upright to make room for her daughter. Each took one end of the tub, pressing the soles of their feet together in between. They leaned back and rested quietly.

That was how the boys found them when they returned from school, one of them yelling "Gross!" as he came in to use the toilet. And that was how Jan found them when she, too, needed the bathroom.

"A person gets no privacy in this house," Jan said, pulling the shower curtain closed. "Run the water, would you?"

Ascending within the ranks, Larry admired the men he met, the men responsible for leadership of the railroad and the companies to which it was closely tied. These were mostly educated men, possessing a sort of confidence and graciousness not common down in the yards. Their generosity with each other surprised Larry.

Once in charge of purchasing for the Great Northern, Larry encountered this generosity in many ways, but Christmastime brought unusual kindnesses. The ringing doorbell filled the Ingerson children with joy because they never knew what gifts awaited. It might have been a towering fruit basket, a box of fine chocolates, a case of good brandy for their father, sweet-smelling European cigarettes for their mother. Or it could have been something really special—a phonograph or a home-movie camera or tickets to the Christmas musical at the Palace. Larry's wife suggested bringing the gifts to the office and sharing them with his staff, but he liked to see the kids so happy. He let them choose which ones he could pass along to others.

In the late fifties, with the railroad under increasing pressure, thanks to the airlines and the automakers, Larry's longtime vendors seemed almost desperate to get his attention, for their bottom line depended on the Great Northern's success. Once, a deliveryman came with an envelope holding a note and a pair of one-hundred-dollar bills. That day, Larry's daughter, Marilyn, had invited over a boy she was seeing, the son of a plumber from the North End. Larry told the boy—Dave was his name—to take the money, to buy something special for his folks. While Larry's teenage son complained, Dave smiled and fumbled to tuck the bills into his wallet.

Jan made dinner that night—her specialty, burgers prepared in the electric frying pan. Marilyn let the other kids keep on watching television, though she knew Dave might be upset to find them lying about when he got home from work. She put Pillsbury biscuits into the oven—a sure bet to please him—and heated some baked beans on the stove.

The table had been set by the time Dave got home. He wore a clean white T-shirt and navy slacks, the heavy-duty sort he liked to buy at Sears. Most of the plumbers wore their coveralls home and cleaned up there, but not Dave. He showered and dressed in the company's backroom because, he'd told Marilyn, he thought it was a poor example to come home in soiled and reeking clothes.

"Ah, golf-ball burgers," he said as Jan set a plateful at the center of the table. "My favorite."

Dave had originated the nickname for the main course. When a pound of ground beef was divided into six equal pieces, the patties were only slightly larger in diameter than a golf ball, and when fried, they rose at the center, taking on a definite roundness. He first used the term as a complaint, but the kids had embraced it with fondness. It was something that marked their family as unlike others. And, really, the burgers weren't half-bad.

"I gather our friend from the government was here today," Dave said.

"How'd you know?" Jan asked.

"When the idiot box is on, the house is a mess, your mother looks like a wreck, and there are golf-ball burgers on the table, I can figure something's wrong," he said.

Marilyn frowned. She sat opposite her husband at the end of the table, which nearly filled the small dining area at the open end of the kitchen. The boys, whispering to each other and lost to the world, sat on one side, the girls on the other. Rosemary, with a cheek full of food, chomped another bite from her burger. Jan watched her mother.

"I'll tell you about it later," Marilyn said.

"Why wait?" Dave's voice had an edge. "Let's hear it."

"Are you upset?" Marilyn asked.

"Not with you," he said, spooning beans onto his plate.

Jan glanced at her father.

Speaking to her, he said, "I only wish your mother hadn't been put in this spot, that we all hadn't. This is Grandpa Larry's trouble, not ours."

"Dave, please," Marilyn said. "Don't involve the kids."

Seeming not to hear her, Dave stared his daughter in the eyes. "His whole life was that railroad. Look what it got him." He punctuated his thought by poking his fork at the tabletop. "Take a lesson from that."

"That reminds me!" Jan was up from the table and out of the room before her parents could comment on her manners. She returned with a book in her hand and sat down. "Just a second. Let me find it."

Marilyn recognized the book—*The Great Gatsby*, required reading in tenth-grade English—although most of the cover was obscured by a large sticker bearing the words "Property of Alexander Ramsey High School." Jan paged around near the back of the book until she found the place.

"Listen to this," she said, but before she began, she looked at her father and explained, "By now Gatsby's been killed and some guy—his dad, I guess—comes to get his body—"

"I think I remember that one," Dave said.

"Okay, then." Jan pressed a finger to the page. "So here it is. He's talking to Gatsby's friend, and the dad says, 'If he'd of lived, he'd of been a great man. A man like James J. Hill. He'd of helped build up the country.'"

Jan closed the book and looked at her parents. The other kids remained oblivious.

"Wild, huh?" Jan said. "I couldn't believe it was in there. Hardly anyone in my class even knew who James J. Hill was."

"Why should they?" Dave said.

The latter years of Larry's career, the ones he had hoped would be a pleasure and a reward, turned out to be the most difficult. He was under constant pressure from above to cut costs, to do ever more with ever less, and his only son was struggling to get a foothold in business out West. He sometimes imagined himself strung between two steam engines pulling mightily in opposing directions.

The railroad was by then under the control of Howard Dunn, a New Yorker who had been lured to St. Paul by Hill descendants and Great Northern board members, all of whom were alarmed by the decline of their company and dreary forecasts for its future. But rather than bringing the business back, Dunn slowly dismantled it, doing away with passenger service and applying tactics on the freight side that were aggressive, cold, and heavy-handed. He undercut competitors—even if it meant short-term operating losses—and promulgated a pricing structure to punish customers who switched to trucking for shorter runs. These changes fractured relationships Larry had built through many years of cooperation and mutual interest.

If not for Charles' trouble in Montana, Larry would have retired sooner and walked away with his friendships and finances in fair shape. But his son had problems he couldn't handle on his own, and Larry wouldn't allow Charles, still a young man, to bankrupt himself and ruin his good name.

Marilyn and Jan were finishing the dishes when Larry walked into the kitchen. They both jumped when he said hello. It was unusual for him to enter their house without ringing the bell.

"Dad!" Marilyn said, her hand over her heart. "What are you doing here?"

Larry kissed Jan's forehead, then did the same to his daughter. "I won't be long," he said. "Grandma sent me to fetch some things from the basement."

Marilyn and her girl exchanged a glance.

"Where are the others?" he asked.

"Out back," Jan said. "Dad's keeping them busy."

They all looked out the window above the sink just in time to see the football bounce off of Rosemary's chest. She picked it up and took off running, her brothers at her heels. Even inside, they heard Dave holler, "Wrong way!" but Rosemary charged ahead toward an imaginary end zone.

Larry said, "I'll just be a minute."

Marilyn let her father go ahead, sent Jan off to do homework, and left the last of the dishes to drip dry. Downstairs, she found him flipping wildly through papers. Drawers yawned open from both file cabinets. Larry sat on the steamer chest and fingered files he drew from the bottom drawer of the nearest cabinet, a drawer marked *Family Records*. He had pushed up the sleeves of his red cardigan and white dress shirt to his elbows. He wore no tie. His thin gray hair—normally parted crisply—fell over his forehead.

"What are you looking for?" Marilyn asked. "What's the matter?"

He finished up with the file and returned it to the drawer. He slammed the drawer shut. Pushed the others in, too. Drew a long breath and wheezed it out through his nose.

"Nothing's here," he said. "I mean, what your mother was looking for isn't here."

Arms crossed over her chest, Marilyn regarded her father and again tried to bring forth the courage to initiate the conversation they needed to have.

"Your mother," he said. "She sent me to look for something from Charles, an old letter. She just doesn't want it lost."

Marilyn found herself speechless.

"It's got nothing to do with that other business," her father said. "It means something to her. She doesn't want it disappearing into a government file somewhere."

Larry followed Marilyn upstairs, and hurried toward the front door. She wanted him to stay awhile, to go out back and say hello to the kids. He refused—no explanation, no hesitation. He was halfway out the front door when Marilyn grabbed his arm.

"Stop, Dad," she said.

He turned back, straddling the threshold, and waited.

She wanted to say just the right thing, to measure her words perfectly so he would understand fully without her needing to speak directly of the matter.

"Dad," she said again. "You realize that if I knew how to help, I would. You know that, right?"

He leaned over to kiss her cheek, whispering, "Don't trouble yourself, sweetheart."

When his son was just a boy, Larry hoped and expected he would go to work for the Great Northern once he was grown, but by the time Charles returned from his time in the navy, both men agreed the rail business was no place for a young man.

Charles went to work for First National Bank, and by the mid-sixties, he had ascended to a private office high up in the bank's downtown tower. His life changed direction, however, after he and his wife took their two girls on a summer trip through the West. They visited Glacier Park, the destination to which the Great Northern once delivered great throngs of

Midwesterners each year, and the beauty of the place left them breathless.

Charles returned with plans to construct a resort in the Montana mountains, just off a new highway, and to build it into something special, a real moneymaker. Larry backed his son with cash, advice, and connections to business associates in the West. Charles built a fine lodge on a mountainside, named it Glacier View, and waited for crowds of travelers to arrive. After three difficult years, Charles' wife took their two girls back to St. Paul, where she moved in with her parents and hoped her husband would come to his senses before going broke entirely.

Larry immediately boarded a freight train headed west and rode along with the crew to Kalispell, where his son met him at the station. Larry stayed only one night at the lodge before advising his son to sell the property and come home, threatening to cut off his subsidies. Charles pleaded for one more year, assuring his father that Glacier View was on the brink of profitability, that he needed only a few last bits of help. Against his better judgment, Larry agreed.

With the kids off to bed and her husband asleep on the sofa, his nose in the fold of Jan's copy of *The Great Gatsby*, Marilyn tiptoed to her room. After easing the door closed, she opened the lowest drawer of her dresser, pulled out a knee-length nightgown—purple cotton, nearly threadbare on the hips—and tossed it onto her bedspread. Then she kneeled and reached deep into the drawer, this time withdrawing an untidy pile of papers.

On the floor, her back against the side of the bed, she paged through the documents. There wasn't much, but it was probably enough. Enough for the IRS man, anyway. At the top of the stack was a letter from Charles, typewritten on the letterhead of Glacier View Lodge, his folly in the West. Marilyn shook her head. Leave it to Charles to waste money on fancy stationary when his business was about to fall into a crevasse. Leave it to Charles to send a typewritten letter to his own father. Leave it to Charles to write:

"I've received the item from your associates, and it has been very helpful. Future prospects for Glacier View enjoy renewed promise, but alas, the short-term challenges have not been resolved entirely. If arrangements could be made for one more item, we would be pleased to accommodate."

This supposedly cryptic slop came from a letter written nearly six years earlier. Marilyn held a dozen others from Charles, all similarly phrased, running right up to the time of their father's retirement. She also had letters from colleagues and friends of her father's that included references—sometimes elliptical, sometimes direct—to the aid they'd provided Glacier View.

Hearing the sound of footsteps from the hallway, she considered stuffing the letters under the bed but didn't move. Dave opened the door and stopped in the frame, looking surprised to see her there—wide awake and sitting on the floor in the dim circle of light from her bedside lamp.

"What are you doing?" he asked, closing the door at his back. "What have you got?"

"I've got what everyone wants," she said, holding up the papers. "Letters from Charles. Dad was trying to save that stupid resort of his."

She handed the letters to her husband, and as he flipped through them, she explained what she could. Marilyn figured it this way: The method by which her father had always done business involved gifts and favors. That was how buyers and sellers showed gratitude and ensured loyalty. But with Charles' resort going broke, her father began asking his colleagues to divert their gestures of goodwill, to send them Charles' way. And as Glacier View's troubles deepened, her father took the next step, trading the railroad's purchasing power for cash gifts to Charles.

"Did your dad give you these?" Dave continued reading as he spoke, turning through the pages and pausing to study bits here and there. When Marilyn didn't answer, he looked her way and said, "Honey, tell me where you got these."

Marilyn reminded him of something Charles' wife had said when she returned from the West, kids in tow, promising never to go back.

"She said the resort would have gone bankrupt long ago if not for Dad's *interference*," Marilyn said. "That was the word she used, *interference*. Naturally, I wondered what she meant."

She made a circular gesture with her hand, meaning *so on and so on*.

"What?" Dave shrugged. "What did you do?"

"This was ages ago, Dave." Marilyn pulled her knees up to her chest. "I went downstairs and had a look. And there it was, plain as day. Big, fat folder marked 'Glacier View.' I wasn't ready for what I found, but we're lucky I went looking."

Now Dave made a circular gesture, which Marilyn took to mean *keep talking, keep talking*. And she did. She explained how she had responded when her father phoned about six months ago to say the IRS wanted to see his personal papers.

"I let Rosie watch TV all day, and I cleaned out those files. I got rid of anything to do with Charles and his ridiculous resort and the friends of Dad's who'd been pulled into it." Marilyn pointed toward the papers in her husband's hands. "That's everything I could find, and I'm pretty sure I found it all."

"Clever girl," Dave said.

He looked at the papers for a moment—then ripped the pile in half, stacked the pieces together, and ripped them in half again. Eyes wide and unblinking, Marilyn watched and smiled. He went on ripping until his cupped hands were filled with small scraps.

After he left the room, she heard the toilet flush. She climbed into the bed and lay on her back, listening to the whine of the pipes as the tank refilled. Another flush came and, eventually, another and another. She thought a plumber ought to know better than to try to send heavy stationary down a toilet, but she appreciated the gesture—the immediacy of his action, its irreversibility.

Once her husband joined her in bed, Marilyn clicked off the lamp and stared up into darkness. She imagined her father in his own bed doing the same thing, waiting for sleep that would be slow to come and thinking about his predicament. She knew it would be a long night, for he must have realized certain papers were missing and concluded they were now in the hands of the IRS. She wished she could reach out—reach all the way across town—and soothe him. She would rest her hand on his face, then brush his hair back off his forehead, and he would go to sleep believing his troubles might pass.

Squirt

I was out behind the tool shed, just trying to sneak a smoke where no one would see, when Hunter, my dead brother's kid, came around the corner and started in again.

"Uncle Pat, what're you doin'?" He squinted in the sunshine, and the skin on his sunburned cheeks looked like it might split. "You promised you'd let me drive the fishin' boat and now you're out here smokin' again. Is that all you're gonna do today?"

There were lots of things I'd like to have said right then, but most weren't the sort you say to your dead brother's boy, considering all the crap the kid's been through already and he's barely seven, especially considering he was there with your brother when some asshole in a Yukon lost control in an inch of snow, went ripping through the median and smacked your brother's minivan—gashed into the driver's door and ripped him right out so when the kid looked for his dad all he saw was a hole and the world whizzing past.

What I could say, the nicest thing I could come up with, was this: "Look, Hunter, I promised I would take you on the boat *today*, not *this morning*, not *this minute*."

It Takes You Over

Hunter stared back at me, his head tilted and mouth hanging open. He stood with his thin little legs squeezed together, said nothing, and kept on staring with that empty look kids have, like he'd been smacked on the forehead. Add to that the lean face and pale skin he inherited from his mother and the permanent cowlick in his mess of blond hair, and Hunter wasn't a terrifically sharp-looking guy. But his eyes were big and trusting, and they could make you ignore a lot of other things.

I didn't know if I'd hurt his feelings or if he couldn't take a hint, but as long as he hung around, I didn't want to take another drag or even flip the ash into the pop can I'd brought along. Smoking in front of little kids always made me uncomfortable, and Hunter's mom, Sarah, used to bust my chops about it nonstop. Sometimes I thought that all she had to say to me was "No shoes on the carpet" and "No smoking in front of Hunter." Right after the accident, she eased up a bit—bigger fish to fry, I guess—but once I showed up at the lake place, she was right back at it.

My brother used to tell me that all I had to do was stand up for myself and Sarah would drop it. I never felt like fighting about it, though, and I didn't see how anything would change. Never mind what Sarah said; I wasn't going to enjoy a smoke in front of Hunter, just as you wouldn't enjoy kissing a girl in front of your mother. That's why I'd slipped out behind the shed while Hunter was supposed to be eating his lunch. I guess I shouldn't have relied on a kid to do what he was supposed to do.

Hunter and I had a little standoff. I let the smoke rise and the ash grow. He watched it closely. We both kept quiet.

Then he broke. He started talking in his odd way, the last word of every sentence drawn out, like he wasn't sure of anything. I watched his eyes, pinched by the brightness, and they stayed right on the cherry and the spent gray ashes hooking downward like a sickle blade. I didn't even know what he was babbling about. I just watched him watching the cig waste away, and I couldn't stand it. I dropped the burning thing into the can and heard it fizz out.

"Are you done now? Can we get goin'?"

"Done?" I said. "I hardly got started. That was like throwing away twenty cents, you know that? Like taking two dimes and throwing them into the lake."

"You didn't have to put it out. I coulda waited. We coulda just talked some more."

Again, there was a huge difference between what I'd like to have said and what I could say to my dead brother's boy. I wanted to say, "Shit, kid, you're killing me. You're breaking my goddamn heart. I'm sorry I'm not a fun guy like your dad. I'm sorry, but I'd rather be alone." But I couldn't.

"Nice offer," I said, "but your mother thinks I'm a bad example. She's probably right. So give me ten minutes, okay? Finish your lunch, round up the life jackets, grab a couple Cokes, and meet me at the dock."

Hunter smiled and sprinted off around the corner. He never walked anywhere; he always ran. Full speed. I'd been with him at the lake for three weeks by then, having driven Up North after I finished my last finals at the U, and I could have sworn the kid only stopped running to shit or sleep. I was happy about that, happy to see that he was still as screwy as any kid, even though all he had for a dad was a bunch of framed photographs propped around the house.

I waited for the slam of the storm door as he went back inside before I torched a fresh one. All that stuff about being a bad role model aside, I couldn't say why I needed a few minutes away from Hunter just then. What I did know was that the whole issue of my smoking was ridiculous and had been for a long time. Trying to hide it was a total failure. I reeked of smoke all the time—never fooled anybody with my mints and gum—and my deceptions seemed to have had a reverse effect on Hunter. Like any kid, he figured the things he wasn't supposed to see or do must be the coolest things in the world.

Last summer, he and some other twerps from his block put on a show. They had cooked up their own play and spent an afternoon practicing so they'd be ready when their folks got home from work. My sister-in-law called and said Hunter wanted me to come over and watch. She didn't invite me, actually. She told me where to be and when to be there. I had crap to do, but Sarah made it sound like it was important that I showed up.

So I drove over to their place and stood around while the moms and dads figured out how to run their camcorders, grinned at each other, and chattered like this was going to be some big deal. Then one of the neighbor dads told us to take our seats, so Sarah and I settled down in a couple lawn chairs, which the kids had lined up in perfect rows on the driveway. We sat facing a closed door on a double garage. My brother joined a few other dads who stood off to the side, ready to roll tape. A neighbor lady shushed everyone, and when it was quiet, she clicked a button on the remote and up went the garage door.

I couldn't really say what the play was about—other than the kids seemed to be searching for an Elmo doll, which had been stolen or kidnapped or some damn thing—but Hunter had an easy role. Right at the start, he shouted, "I'm Uncle Pat," and then he pulled a three-inch piece of drinking straw from his pocket, jammed it into the crook of his fingers, raised it to his lips, and sucked like he was trying to draw a golf ball through a garden hose. The moms and dads hooted, except for Sarah, who flashed me a look as hard as a punch in the gut. I saw my brother swing his camcorder around to catch my reaction. I smiled and played it off okay, but I felt like an idiot. I wanted to whisper a bit of apology to Sarah, but I couldn't think of what to say.

And for the rest of the play—which wasn't much more than five minutes or so—Hunter said nothing more. He just stood there in his baggy shorts and dirty T-shirt with his arms crossed and that plastic straw dangling from his lips. It was funny and cutesy, I suppose. Part of me felt good that Hunter liked me and maybe looked up to me, but another part of me couldn't help thinking, *Jesus Christ, kid, is that all I am to you, just a jerk with a heater in his hand?*

After the show ended and the kids took their bows, my brother said, "He nailed you pretty good."

"You probably put him up to that," I said, "Or was it Sarah's idea?"

"We had nothing to do with it." He had a half-smile on his face, which he often did when we talked and which made me wonder sometimes if he thought I was funny—or a joke. "We'd never interfere with the artistic process."

"Well," I said, "at least your kid knows style when he sees it."

I was kidding, but my brother didn't laugh. He patted my shoulder like he was consoling me, and then he wandered off to talk with the other dads. I decided one thing: It was time to be straight with Hunter. My sneaking around wasn't fooling him, so I figured I'd let him see me smoking, let him know what I was really like—the real me. I planned to tell him the truth about how I woke up with a headache every day and how I'd have quit that second if only I'd had the stones to stick with it. But I never had a chance to give that speech, never went through with it before everything changed and nothing that had seemed important before mattered much anymore.

The summer breezed by, fall came and went, and one day my brother went out on the road during some November flurries. It was right after Thanksgiving. He was headed for Home Depot to pick up some paint for Hunter's bedroom, and he took the kid along for the ride. They'd moved into a new house that year. All the walls were white. Everything was clean and perfect. My brother wasn't even thirty years old, but he had started his own mortgage company. He always knew how to make a buck. His wife was pretty in her own way. His kid was happy. Everything was about right. And then, smack.

It Takes You Over

Half a year later and there I was, all alone and sucking down a cig behind the rusting tool shed that stands beside our family's lake place—where my brother and I had passed a lot of summer days, where he'd tried and failed to teach me to water-ski worth a damn, and where his wife and son were now passing time. I only wanted a few minutes to myself. I guess I needed to let my mind go blank, to stop thinking about all the horrible shit I couldn't stop thinking about whenever I was around Sarah and Hunter. But then the kid had to come out, and even when I sent him away, he was all I had on my mind.

I couldn't imagine what happens inside a kid's head when he goes through something like Hunter went through—when he sees his dad wiped out and then has to spend the next hour with some lady paramedic while the cops try to track down his family. Thinking of what happened after the crash drove me crazy. What did the kid see first? Was it the shiny steel of the minivan's torn-up frame? The broken glass, highway slush, and ditch mud blown in through shattered windows and the huge hole in the van's body? The red of the lights on cop cars, ambulances, fire trucks? The strange face of the person who unbuckled him and pulled him from the backseat?

Then what happened? What did those people say to him? What did Hunter say? How much did he know or even understand?

Those sixty slow minutes couldn't be changed. They were all gone, and I knew that. But I wanted to find out everything Hunter saw, everything he thought, every bit of fear and kindness he experienced. I wished I'd been there beside him. A thing like that should have been shared. When I was a kid, bad things were always easier when I had someone with me. Then I could say one word about it, and that person would know exactly what I meant. Sometimes I thought of asking Hunter to tell me all about it, but you don't dig up things like that with a kid. You let him be. You help him along. You listen if he talks.

I took a long, slow drag on my cigarette, which made me feel as if I wanted to puke or cry or both. So I sat down, shut

Squirt

my eyes, tilted my face to the sky, and blasted the smoke out through my nostrils. As I leaned my head against the shed wall, which had warmed in the morning sun, I listened to the sounds of the lakeshore—waves against the sand, a weak breeze through the leaves, and the buzz of an outboard pushing along some stranger's boat far in the distance. I might have stayed like that all day.

The clang of dishes from inside the house told me Hunter would be along again soon—back in my face with his *Aw, Uncle Pat, c'mon, c'mon, c'mon.* I sat up, blinked my eyes clear, and realized I was sort of looking forward to it. The storm door squealed and slammed again, but Hunter didn't come my way. I heard him bounce onto the dock and start knocking around in the fishing boat. I knew Sarah wouldn't want him down there alone, so I slipped the remaining bit of my cigarette into the soda can and gave it a shake.

The ground beneath me was still cool and damp from night-time showers, and I could feel moisture seeping through the fabric of my shorts and onto my skin. It was a sensation that normally would have made me uncomfortable and sort of mad at nobody in particular, but for some reason, it pleased me at the moment. I realized it didn't matter if I walked around with a big wet stain on my ass. That was the bright side of my situation. I hadn't meant to spend the summer as a stand-in for my dead brother—to leave my friends, my stuff, and my life behind, take over the extra room in the lake house, and let his kid follow me around all day. But that's how it turned out, and at least I didn't have to worry about how I looked or what anybody thought about me. I could do no wrong in Hunter's eyes, and Sarah had too much on her mind to give a crap about me, other than complaining about my smoking, which was just her nature. I knew where I stood, and that was good.

When I got up and stepped around the corner of the shed, I spotted Hunter at the back of the fishing boat, his hand twisting and twisting at the outboard's throttle. His puckered lips vibrated, and though I couldn't hear the put-put of his little pretend motorboat, I knew its sound. I whistled to get his attention, and the kid freaked. He scrambled over the middle bench, then plopped down in the front of the boat and looked around like he'd been there all along.

"Hey," I yelled. "It's okay. Knock yourself out. I'll be there in a couple minutes."

He didn't say anything, so I yelled again.

"Two minutes, Hunter. Give me two minutes."

I stepped back behind the shed and smoked one more cigarette all the way down to the filter. I smoked it hard and fast—and paced, trying to shake off the weight of all that bad stuff I'd been thinking about. I tried to get myself feeling light and mellow, so Hunter wouldn't peg me as another one of those grown-ups in his life still slouching around with that look of helpless misery we all wore at the funeral and during the days before and after. I drew one last drag, held the smoke in my lungs, stomped the butt into the ground, and blew out a tight stream of gray smoke, which spread into the sunshine and disappeared.

I felt pretty good by the time I trotted across the yard and onto the dark sand of the beach. Hunter still sat in the bow of the fishing boat, facing the rear like a good passenger. He smiled real wide when he saw me coming, and that made me feel even better. He had his orange life jacket clipped on tight. Two cans of pop lay on top of a crumpled beach towel at his feet, just as I'd told him. While I untied the first line from the post, he leaned over and moved the Cokes aside. I threw off the second rope, climbed down into the boat, and sat on the rear bench.

"You ready for some high-speed cruisin'?" I asked.

Hunter didn't say a word.

I looked up and found myself staring straight down the barrel of his new squirt gun, not one of those wimpy deals I had as a kid but a huge neon-colored Super Soaker things, where the kid pumps it up and lets fly. I sensed Hunter had done the pumping in advance. The enormous shit-eating grin on his face gave that much away.

"Don't do it, Hunter," I said. "Not if you think I'm going to let you steer this—"

The stream went into my mouth like he was playing a carnival game, and when I closed my lips and turned my head, the water roared into my ear and drenched my hair, my cheek, my neck, my T-shirt. Hunter laughed until I leaned forward to jerk the squirt gun from his hands.

I was too forceful, pulling him clear off his seat before he let go and tumbled backward.

"You little snot," I said. "You're lucky I don't—"

Then I didn't know what to say. We froze like that, him wide-eyed with the metal edge of the bench pressed into his back and me holding a pink-and-yellow squirt gun and letting water drip from my face. What I wanted to say was, "Why did you have to spoil this? You've been after me all morning, and you're about to get what you want. So what do you do? You ruin it, ruin the whole damn day." But even as pissed as I was, I knew I couldn't say that.

I raised the barrel of the gun, pumped a couple times, and squeezed the trigger. A thin stream spurted onto Hunter's leg, then only air. He hooted and howled.

"Empty!" He laughed so hard he couldn't speak another word.

I grabbed him under the armpits, lifted him high, and hurled his bony frame over the edge of the boat and into the lake. He spat and coughed when he came up, but also smiled and laughed between coughs. Then he whirled and swung one arm across the surface, sending a huge splash into the boat and onto me.

I didn't know what else to do, so I jumped in after him. In midair, I thought about the pack of cigarettes in my pocket, but it was too late to save them. When I caught up to Hunter, I lifted him up, put one hand under his tailbone, and launched him skyward the way I'd seen my brother do a hundred times in this very lake on days just like this but like we'd never have again.

My brother's boy jackknifed into the water and came up wild-eyed and ready for more.

He screamed, "You're dead, Uncle Pat."

His little legs churned the water until I let him catch me and drag me down. His fingernails gouged my skin as we rolled into the water, still clear and cold early in the season, and he wrapped his legs around me. He clung hard to my back, but I found my balance, rose, and bucked him off. He crashed down, flailed underwater, and came up laughing again. We splashed and dunked each other until his mother came out of the house and hollered for us to stop.

Uncle Ed's Packard

Duck hunters always left the keys on the dash or in the ashtray or, if they weren't the trusting sort, under the floor mat. Safer that way than bringing them along and getting them lost if you tripped in the brush or, heaven forbid, tipped the boat. Farrell found the keys in Uncle Ed's Packard, a smart-looking but temperamental black sedan that Ed had gone all the way to St. Paul to buy. Before turning the ignition, Farrell pressed the gas pedal three times, just as Ed always did, and implored the motor to cooperate.

Daylight had broken warm and bright, but by mid-morning things turned November-typical, chilly mist coming down and gray skies all around. Farrell had come four miles on foot, figuring he'd drive over to Nicollet to scoop up Lenora for half a day and get the car back before Ed and his friend stumbled out of the woods with bags full of bleeding redheads and bellies full of schnapps. Rain had dampened Farrell's yellow hair and his neck, and seeped into his coat, leaving him an aching back and dripping nose. The skin on Farrell's knuckles was wet and red. The Packard's motor rattled and wheezed. Farrell let off, cursed, and blew into cupped hands. After one more gentle touch of gas, he cranked the key again. The car awakened with a roar.

"Thank you," Farrell whispered. He couldn't be ashamed of this. He and his mother had no car of their own, and he needed to do some living, after all. He smiled, revved the engine, and fingered a switch on the dash. He mumbled, "Let's have some heat."

Ed and his crony hunted the same place each year. They left their car parked halfway in the ditch, hiked a short bit through brush along Swift Lake, and rowed eastward to a small island at the mouth of a marshy bay. Sometimes birds swept through that way by the score, and the hunters could fire over the cattails from boats or from shore. An old lean-to with a wood floor gave the men a place to escape the wind, swap stories, and sip from their bottles.

"Figure this rain'll quit?" Ed asked his friend.

"Not on your life," said the man, known to most only as Kowalska. He liked to tell people he was Polack-Sioux, and with one look at him, no one doubted it.

Kowalska worked in the limestone quarry outside Mankato; all the men did. Ed and his brother gave up the Nebraska dust years ago and moved their families where there was work. The quarry was the first place willing to have them.

"Better warm up with a toot," Kowalska said.

Not so far west, clouds had coiled themselves into something fierce, and winds drove rainfall against farmhouses and barns and livestock in the pasture. Cold air whooshed earthward, and the season seemed to change in a lone mighty gust. Rain froze against white clapboards, red planks, and matted brown fur. Ahead of the wind, skies darkened with throngs of birds. Ducks by the thousand beat their wings and chased warmth as this new fierce thing swept out of the Dakotas and across the fields of Minnesota.

Lenora waited in the doorway of Stoney's Saloon, her father's place. Leaning her forehead against the glass, she watched for the car Farrell had described, a big and beautiful black Packard. Farrell had an adventurous side. He was the sort of guy who'd steal his uncle's car just to drive you around so you could be alone together and maybe stop awhile down on the riverbottom road.

The rain and wind looked to be picking up, but Lenora didn't feel like changing out of her skirt. The morning began with such sunshine and warmth, and there'd been no work to do. The whole town shut down for the Armistice Day remembrance. Her father had left before sunrise to hunt, so she enjoyed time to herself, even opening windows to let in the gentle air. She'd dressed for that weather, and now her only concession to the rain was a hip-length coat, left unbuttoned.

"What's in that purse?" Farrell asked first thing after Lenora locked up, ran to the curb, and let herself into the car.

"Is that how you say hello?" Lenora asked.

Even with a cross expression on her face, Lenora looked great to Farrell. She was a fine girl, he thought. She had blond hair, which she always pushed behind her ears, and her lashes were so light they were nearly invisible. Farrell patted her leg. "I meant 'Hello, darling, what's in there?'"

She smiled, held open her bag, and showed him the two bottles of beer and a silver flask. She closed the purse and slid over next to Farrell. He hit the accelerator and, after they'd passed the western limit of town, crooked his arm over her shoulders.

Birds to the rear beat their wings desperately, somehow knowing they were just ahead of trouble. In front of them flew waves and waves of ducks and geese, everything that had been headed south, and a loose haze of local birds, stirred up from daily routines and scared into flight. Many swooped low in the river valley and followed its southeasterly path, ditching out of prairie gusts and taking advantage of the steadier tailwind coursing through the wide valley.

Farrell guided the Packard slowly along the gravel road leading toward the river, where they could cruise in the bottoms and find a quiet spot to stop for a beer and a talk, or whatever else they dared—never much. Lenora sipped from the flask and held it to Farrell's lips, tipping it up when he gave a little nod. He steered with his left arm and kept his right around her.

"Tastes good," Farrell said. "I like that warmth in my throat."

"Me too," she said. "I love how you can feel it spreading down from your tongue to the bottom of your stomach. It takes you over."

Rain, falling ever harder, slapped against the windshield and swooshed away on the wipers. Farrell told Lenora to hold the wheel, which she did while he fumbled with switches until the wipers sped to a frantic pace.

"There," he said, taking the wheel again. "Now I can see something."

"I like this car," Lenora said. "It's a nice one."

Farrell steered onto the riverside hill. Down below glowed the headlights of a car creeping upward. Lenora slid to the side, and Farrell put both hands on the wheel, rode the brakes, and kept over as far as possible. Lenora turned her face away when the car passed, but Farrell gave a wave. The

Uncle Ed's Packard

man driving the rattletrap of a Ford waved back; the three men with him nodded.

"Just a sorry flock of old hunters," Farrell said. "Don't worry."

"I hope no one recognized me," Lenora said, scooting back to the seat's middle. "My father'll blow steam if he hears I was out here with you."

Two counties over, Lenora's father stood alone in the river sloughs where long ago his father and grandfather had taught him to hunt. Birds passed overhead like puffs of wind-driven smoke off a prairie fire. Thick blots of crows swirled by, going like the ducks, going like every flying thing. He wondered about this, wondered what those other birds were doing and why migrating flocks were following a path more east than south. He wondered what his father and grandfather would've made of it.

Farrell tasted bourbon on Lenora's lips, smelled it in her breath, felt it in his eyes. With the Packard idling in a pull-off on the bottom road, they kissed and Farrell moved a hand under her coat and over the soft cotton of her blouse, cupping his hand and feeling the form of her. He was nearly eighteen and had never seen a real woman out of her clothes. He didn't know how that was ever going to change.

When they'd kissed for as long as seemed reasonable, they stopped and looked at the brown river, its current carrying long naked branches and curled golden leaves. She suggested they drink the beers before they got warm. One at a time he wedged the bottle tops under the window crank and popped them off.

Two weeks short of a year had passed since Farrell's father went deer hunting up north and never came back. He'd been

It Takes You Over

sharing a rented cabin with Lenora's father, Uncle Ed, and some others. The night before they were due to come home, Farrell's father drove to town for cigarettes. No one had seen him since. First there was a fuss, as if perhaps he'd driven off the road somewhere or gotten lost and run dry of fuel. But soon everyone whispered the likelier truth—he'd just run. Not long after, Lenora's mother left for a shopping trip and never came back.

Sitting along the river in the Packard, the heater working away and windows half-fogged, Farrell looked at Lenora. They'd passed a lot of time together since their folks ran off, and they'd pretty well talked the matter into the ground. But Farrell hadn't mentioned one thing: There'd been silence at the family table one night shortly before his father's hunting trip. Farrell's father had looked at his mother and said, "Do you ever stop and think: What if I've been wrong?"

Farrell's mother didn't look up from her plate, so Farrell said, "Wrong about what?"

His father, who seemed a little drunk, said, "Wrong about everything."

As Farrell considered how to begin, Lenora leaned forward and wiped the windshield with the cuff of her coat. She narrowed her eyes, leaned close to the glass. Farrell looked that way too and saw a black swirl in the sky, like smoke, pouring toward them. Lenora said, "What's that?"

A ways upstream, a dozen steers had gone down a slope in their riverside pasture. The animals wanted only to move with the wind. They trudged away from their barn, toward barbed wire above a creek, which flowed into the river and formed the southeast corner of the farmer's property. The rain fell and fell; the temperature fell and fell. Water soaking their brown hides glazed in the cold. Rain turned to sleet. Ice held one steer's eyelids together until the bellowing animal shook his head and forced them open. Sleet turned to snow, which came in coarse waves, like wind-whipped sand. The steers crowded, hemmed in by wire, their backs still to the wind and snow.

Farrell pulled Lenora his way, and she kneeled across his lap, her backside wedged against the steering wheel, as they kissed with renewed energy. The sight of all those birds and the thrumming as they passed overhead stirred something inside the pair. Farrell figured they'd been graced by luck, getting that chance to be alone together while witnessing something so unusual, something amazing and awesome. He could tell Lenora knew it too, and he thought this might bind them.

Both hands inside her coat, Farrell explored her soft places and the bulging contours where undergarments pressed into flesh. He ran one hand down her back, around her curve, along the underside of her thigh. His fingers brushed the skin of her calf. He rested his hand in the crook of her knee.

Washes of rain on the roof mixed with the hum of the engine. Wind clattered branches above and whistled against the windshield. The birds had mostly passed. Farrell wanted to look—to see her face and her body and everything happening, but he forced his eyes closed, knowing the polite way. He kept his eyelids pressed together until he heard what sounded like someone throwing handfuls of dirt against the steel and glass of the Packard.

Several dull, cold hours after the men had fanned their decoys on the water, dozens of ducks came dropping in. They came so quick and low that Ed yelled out, "Better watch your cap!" He laughed and blasted away, wasting hardly any birdshot, always knocking down something. After midday, Ed and Kowalska reached their limit of ten apiece, and they'd been celebrating with the schnapps. Growing gusts drove across Swift Lake from the west and into the hunters' faces.

Ed looked back over the lake, his eyes watering, and considered the return trip to the car. The duckboat, which he'd built himself, was a miserably unsteady thing. The lake chopped. Waves rolled up over the spines of smaller ones ahead. The row back would be short, a few hundred yards. But still, he thought.

"We'd better beat it out of here if we get a break in the wind," Ed said.

Kowalska, a wide-bellied man with an arrowhead nose, peered westward. He must have seen what Ed saw. With one arm cradling the stock of his lowered gun, Kowalska said, "I say we go before it gets worse."

Snow came in wind-driven waves; it came with violence in it. To Farrell's eyes, the birds had moved like smoke, dark and swirling smoke, but he couldn't make sense of snow like this. There was power in its impact on the windshield, and some of it adhered there, glazing the glass in seconds. He ran the wipers, but they skittered on icy patches. Farrell and Lenora fell back against the seat and watched the sudden storm outside, where whiteness coated the west sides of the brown tree trunks and coated the brown earth, and where the brown vein of the river could hardly be seen through waves of white.

"It's like a dust storm," Farrell said.

Farrell remembered Nebraska's dust—how it blasted against the house, how people stuffed sheets and rags around doors and windows to keep the black out, but after a few years as a town boy in southern Minnesota, that seemed another life.

"See what Ed's got in the glove box, would you?" Farrell messed with switches and waved fingers over the dashboard vent while Lenora rifled through the compartment and withdrew a chipped razor blade.

"Is this all he's got?" she asked, but Farrell didn't answer. He clasped the blade between two fingers, pulled the door handle, and held his coat closed with his free hand. As he stepped out, wind buffeted the door and banged it on his shin. He let out a curse and lowered a shoulder to push the door wide. The noise and chill of the wind shocked him, took the breath from his lungs. He had no cap or gloves. Standing on the running board and leaning across the hood, he worked the blade against the ice, clearing first a small square and scratching until he'd bared a decent patch of glass.

A gale whipped over Swift Lake after the massive flight of birds dissipated. Ed and Kowalska had all the decoys pulled in, all their kills tossed into the duckboat, their guns and gear piled here and there. The wind came hard now, gusts so cold and strong they scorched the skin.

Kowalska cut two holes in a gunnysack and pulled it over his head, over his arrowhead nose. He stepped into the front of the boat and sat low in its bottom. His job was to be ballast and to bark directions while Ed would work the oars. Ed pushed the boat out, kicked a leg up, and hoisted himself onto the middle seat.

"Now or never," Ed said as he pulled on the oars, inching the boat away from the island. He had to holler to be heard over the wind. His boat headed straight into the teeth of the whitecaps.

The Packard fishtailed up the muddy, snowy hill that led from the river bottom to the country road. Farrell exhaled once they'd crested the hill, but once out of the valley's protection, he found it hard to distinguish the white sky from the dust-like white blowing over the roadway. Lenora leaned against the dash and used her palm to rub fog from the glass in front of the steering wheel.

"That's good," Farrell said. "That helps."

If he kept it to fifteen miles an hour, he could clearly see the flat of the road ahead and dim shadows of ditches. At twenty, he could see less but well enough. At twenty-five, he had to call on instinct. Having the wind at his back helped, although snow streamed past almost parallel to the ground and tricked Farrell's eyes. He gripped the steering wheel and concentrated, keeping a reasonable speed.

"My father'll go wild if I'm not there when he gets home," Lenora said.

"Where was he hunting?"

"Out near his old place in Renville County," she said.

"He's got a longer drive than we do." Farrell looked at Lenora for an instant, recognizing anxiety in the squint of her eyes. Her father had gone two counties west, where the storm must have stirred up earlier. "He'll stay put there until this passes."

"He's probably calling on the telephone right now." Lenora rubbed her hand over the glass again. "He'll just go wild."

Ed and the gunnysacked Kowalska dragged the duckboat onto land and grabbed their guns and packs. The cold would keep the ducks just fine. When Ed looked back across the water, he saw only a gray form behind the snow, a shadow in the shape of the island's stubble of trees.

"Let's go, Ed!" Kowalska said.

They lowered their heads and moved off through the scraggly woods near the lakeshore. They emerged into the open field and trotted over matted grass, which had soaked up rain and now, quickly being covered by snow, crackled under their boots. Ed squinted toward the road, but snow and wind seared his eyes. After yanking a collar over his face, he stole a quick look and wondered how he could be missing it. His Packard should be right there.

Farrell felt the car veering into the ditch, never saw the roadside but felt shudders as the tires rumbled off the grade. He fought to hold steady. Lenora yelped, but his concentration held. He didn't jerk the wheel. He didn't hit the brakes. He let off the gas and let the Packard bounce along. A wake of slush kicked up to the right. With a leftward lean, Farrell eased the car back squarely onto gravel.

"That's good," Lenora said. "Just go slow."

"We'll be lucky to make it to Nicollet," Farrell replied.

"You have to stay until this passes." Lenora still bent forward, ready to wipe the glass. The heater fan whirred, but the air in the car held a chill. "Your uncle could walk home sooner than you could drive over to that lake."

"If I could even keep on the road." Farrell had slowed the Packard to barely better than a crawl. "What'll we say if your dad's back at the bar?"

"We'll say we were out hunting—" Lenora began.

"For the lovebirds," said Farrell.

The couple laughed, dark laughter. What else could they do? Farrell wanted to reach for Lenora right then, to pull her close, but he kept his hands on the wheel and his eyes ahead. If there were things worth fearing, this storm was among them. Soon he spotted something in the horizon shadows—the spire of a church, the hulk of a grain elevator, the shape of Lenora's town.

Ed ran up and down the roadside, spitting curses and searching for any sign of his car. Blowing snow rendered him practically blind. He craned his neck to keep his face out of the wind and scanned for tire tracks or footprints. He cursed at the snow-covered mud, gravel, and grass. Kowalska stood, his back to the wind, and tried to rub warmth into his cheeks.

"It's gone!" Ed slapped his thighs. "The car is gone. How can that be?"

"What'll we do now?" Kowalska asked. "We'd have been better off in the lean-to."

Farrell and Lenora drank coffee mixed with whiskey and looked through the window at the empty street in front of Stoney's Saloon. They'd parked the Packard around back and braced for trouble as they climbed the stairs to Lenora's apartment. But they found the place empty, and after failed attempts to get phone calls through and to pick up anything on the radio, they'd accepted their isolation. Not a soul was about in Nicollet, a slow town even on a good day.

Lenora had changed into warm clothes, and they'd gone down to the bar, made their drinks, and sat at a table near the front window. Snow piled on the street, and they watched the blizzard work. The drink warmed Farrell's chest and calmed him. He couldn't help but feel a moment of happiness—to be there with Lenora, safe and alone and hidden from the rest of the world. Trouble would come from this day, but he assured himself that Ed would be just fine. Sure he would.

"I opened windows this morning," Lenora said. "That's how warm it felt."

"We almost ditched the Packard," Farrell said. "And you with your skirt and flimsy shoes."

Lenora rolled her eyes and smiled. They looked into the dark gray of the afternoon light, where a lamppost out front

Uncle Ed's Packard

swayed in the wind. They listened to the snarl of steady gusts, to the snow and ice crystals striking the window glass, and to the sound of their own breathing. Their thoughts drifted.

"Where do you think they are?" she asked.

Farrell didn't have to ask.

"I don't care anymore," he said.

"You'd think they'd at least send a letter." Lenora slouched and crossed her arms over her chest, sweater bunching under her chin.

"I hope he's out in a duck blind somewhere, freezing his tail," Farrell said.

When Lenora went off to bed, he lay down on the sofa. He thought it best to keep his coat on, in case her father turned up. No telling how that old hothead might react. Weary but fitful, Farrell thought about Lenora asleep in her room, the warmth of her tongue, the things he felt through her clothes. He thought, too, about his mother alone at home, his uncle stuck out there.

And out there in the ceaseless wind and numbing cold were things he couldn't have imagined—cows with mud hardening around their hooves and ice encasing their nostrils, turkeys freezing together in bulging clots, and hunters hunkering anywhere they could hide from the wind. Farrell had no idea. He closed his eyes and listened for stirring in Lenora's room, hearing only the storm swirl outside as he finally drifted off.

Soon after daybreak, he went to the window and squinted at the white earth under blue sky. He checked the back and saw a white mound where he'd left the Packard. He put an ear to Lenora's bedroom door, then went downstairs to the bar, poured a glass of water, and sat at the front table.

Later he would learn how Uncle Ed and Kowalska had trudged up the road through ever-deepening snow, how they'd made it two full miles, how they'd gone right past a farmhouse drive. But that morning he knew only that nothing outside was moving, that nobody but Lenora had any idea where he was. For a time he was lost to the world, and he liked the feeling, the easy freedom of it.

Acknowledgments

These stories have appeared in various forms in the following publications:

"Joyless Men" in *Water-Stone Review*, *The 2008 Robert Olen Butler Prize Stories*, and *Tartts: Incisive Writing from Emerging Writers*
"Uncle Ed's Packard" in *Minnesota Monthly*
"Ashes and Spit" in *North American Review*
"And Other Delights" in *Speakeasy*
"Squirt" in *Blueroad*
"Close Relations" and "Lives of Great Northerners" in *Great River Review*

My thanks to the many friends and fellow writers whose advice and encouragement supported the creation of these stories, especially Nate LeBoutillier, Nicole Helget, Thomas Maltman, Aaron Frisch, and Michael O'Hearn; to the creative writing faculty at Minnesota State University, Mankato, especially Roger Sheffer, Richard Robbins, and Terry Davis; to Robert Hedin at the *Great River Review*; to everyone at the Anderson Center in Red Wing, MN; to John Gaterud at Blueroad Press; to Sheila O'Connor at *Water-Stone Review*; to the staff at New Rivers Press; to the late poet Dorothy Nordstrom; to Micky and Bob Ferguson of St. Paul, MN; and to my wife, Helen, and our children, Harry and Erin.

Special thanks to author Joan Connor, the final judge who chose this collection and helped make this book possible.

Author Biography

Readers were introduced to Nick Healy's fiction when "And Other Delights" was chosen for the 2005 Speakeasy Prize from The Loft Literary Center/*Speakeasy* magazine. Since then Healy's stories have found an audience in the Midwest and across the country. His work has appeared in magazines including *North American Review*, *Broken Bridge Review*, *Water-Stone Review*, *Minnesota Monthly*, *Blueroad*, and *Great River Review*, and his stories have been anthologized in *The Robert Olen Butler Prize Stories* (Del Sol Press), *Tartts Four: Incisive Fiction* (Livingston Press), and *Blink Again: Sudden Fiction from the Upper Midwest* (Spout Press).

It Takes You Over, Healy's first collection of short stories and New Rivers Press' 125th Many Voices Project award winner, was written with the support of an Artist Initiative Grant from the Minnesota State Arts Board and a McKnight Individual Artist Grant from Prairie Lakes Regional Arts Council.

A native of St. Paul, Healy now lives in Mankato, Minnesota, with his wife, Helen, and their two children.